Supercouple

Other Books by Mary Towne

PAUL'S GAME

Supercouple

Mary Towne

7724

DELACORTE PRESS / NEW YORK

Published by
Delacorte Press
1 Dag Hammarskjold Plaza
New York, N.Y. 10017

MANUFACTURED IN THE UNITED STATES OF AMERICA
FIRST PRINTING

Library of Congress Cataloging in Publication Data

Towne, Mary.
  Supercouple.
  Summary: A cheerleader and a football player begin
a relationship that is the envy of their peers, but
they come to realize they don't really know each other
at all.
  I. Title.
PZ7.T6495Su 1985   [Fic]
ISBN 0-385-29379-8
Library of Congress Catalog Card Number: 84–16961

1

"There she is!"

"Binky! Hey, Binky, wait up!"

"I can't wait to see her face when she *hears,* can you?"

When the cheerleaders bore down on her, Bianca Rosemary Nolan had just come out of the school library and was looking up at the new bronze sign above the doors. LI-BRARY, it read, replacing MEDIA CENTER. The new principal was said to be a conservative type. Since no one had ever called the library the media center anyway, this seemed like a sensible move to Binky. She wondered if it really was a new sign or just an old one that had been lying around in the basement somewhere during the media center years.

The thought made her smile, and the cheerleaders slowed their pace.

"Maybe she already knows," someone said, sounding disappointed.

"How could she, when we only just now took a vote?" This was Donna Sprague, the tall blonde. Or no, not

Donna, Binky corrected herself—Doro, short for Dorothy. She seemed to remember Miss Walker's saying that Doro was the head cheerleader.

"Binky, guess *what?*"

Binky looked into the eager snub-nosed face of Sue Streibeck, the only cheerleader she really knew—they'd been in Brownies together, and fourth grade, and seventh— and suppressed a sigh. Even if Miss Walker hadn't practically said that Binky was a sure thing, Binky figured she'd have to be pretty dense not to have guessed by now what the big news was.

But she said, "What?" obediently.

"You're on the squad—the senior squad! Miss Walker decided not to hold new tryouts after all. She's afraid it might mess up the junior squad, because practically all of them wanted to try out for Cathy's spot, only they're already working really well as a unit, you know?" Binky thought she recognized a direct quote from Miss Walker. "Of course, what she'll *say* is that there just wasn't enough time to audition everyone who signed up. Which is true, actually, when you think of Homecoming next weekend and everything.

"Anyway"—Sue paused for breath—"she just gave us a list of names to pick from, and . . . well, I probably shouldn't tell you what the vote was, but—"

"Oh, come on, Sue," Doro interrupted, flicking back her mane of wheat-colored hair in a gesture familiar to hundreds of Cameron High sports fans, if not to Binky, who never went to games. "She might as well know we didn't even have to think twice. The minute we found out Binky was interested . . ." She shrugged. "I mean, who could be more perfect to take over Cathy's spot? She's even the right type."

Short, dark, and vaguely Italian-looking, Binky assumed

she meant, like Cathy Rubino, the defecting cheerleader, who had a bad case of mono. But of course there was a good deal more to it than that, considering that Binky knew nothing whatever about cheerleading. It was her gymnastic ability they'd pounced upon—the years of training and competition which still enabled Binky to do a standing tuck or a series of back handsprings without even thinking about it. Even though she'd quit gymnastics two years ago, Binky still worked out regularly, mostly to keep in shape, in the makeshift gym her father had set up in the basement when she was nine.

Caroline Horner said in her cool voice, "When we saw your name on the sign-up sheet, we thought it must be a mistake, or a joke or something. I mean, you've never exactly been into school things, have you, Binky? But as Doro says, when Miss Walker told us you were really serious . . ."

That was how Miss Walker had begun, too—picking the sign-up sheet from her desk and saying, "This *is* your handwriting, I presume, Binky? Not just someone playing a practical joke?" When Binky shook her head, Miss Walker gave her a long look and said, "Well, well. Wonders never cease. Of course you'd be a great addition to the squad. Ability *and* personality." She sighed. "When I think of all the girls who'd just love to spend their Saturday afternoons jumping up and down in front of a crowd in a cute little skirt and sweater . . . There's a good deal more to cheerleading than that, as I trust you realize, Binky."

"Well, sure," said Binky, who hadn't. "I mean, I know there'll be a lot of things to learn. The chants, and all that."

"The chants." Miss Walker leaned back in her chair and contemplated her in silence for a moment. Then she said, "Binky, I don't think you have the slightest idea what you're getting into. More than that, I don't understand *why* this sudden interest in cheerleading, considering that up to now you've made no contribution to the school whatever that I know of."

Binky was about to protest that she'd helped with layouts for the yearbook last year, and sold tickets for the variety show, and that it was, after all, only the beginning of her junior year. But of course she'd already said all those things to Spencer, who'd only laughed at her—who, in fact, had made her so mad that she'd gone storming off to the main bulletin board in the front hall, ready to sign herself up for the Madrigal Singers or the Quilting Society, if necessary. It was a lucky thing the cheerleader vacancy had caught her eye, she thought now.

But she supposed she'd better not tell Miss Walker any of that. It might sound a bit casual, she was beginning to realize. Instead, she said earnestly, "Well, I've decided I want to get involved, Miss Walker. To . . . you know, show school spirit. And cheerleading just seemed like something I might be able to do." Which was no more than the truth. Besides, Binky thought in satisfaction, Spencer could talk all he liked about the responsibility of editing the school paper, but who demonstrated school spirit more dramatically than a cheerleader, out there in the wind and weather, cheering the team on to victory?

"Oh, you'll be able to *do* it, all right," Miss Walker assured her. There was an odd little glint in her eye. "And as for involvement—well, I don't think you'll have any complaints on that score, Binky. In fact, the main thing that concerns me is that you understand just how much time and effort you'll have to put in, off the playing field as well as on it."

"Oh, I do, Miss Walker," Binky told her, but rather absently; Miss Walker's reference to the playing field had awakened her one real doubt. "The only thing is . . ."

"Yes?"

"Well, about the games themselves, that we'll be cheering at . . . Miss Walker, I guess you should know that I've only ever been to one football game in my whole life. And I didn't like it at all. Well, I guess that doesn't matter too much," Binky added hastily, in case this sounded rude, "but the point is, I don't understand the rules. And later on there'll be basketball, and that's even crazier. I'm afraid I'll never catch on to that. So what worries me is—well, how will I ever know when to cheer?"

"Binky . . ." Miss Walker took a deep breath, then seemed to change her mind about whatever she was going to say. "Basketball is easy," she said in a firm voice. "Every time one of our players sends the ball through the hoop, you cheer. Unless he fouls someone, of course." Binky shook her head doubtfully, and Miss Walker sighed. "Well, never mind about the rules, Binky. Just watch the other girls. Or for that matter, just listen to the *crowd,* for heaven's sake."

As Binky opened her mouth, Miss Walker said quickly, "Yes, yes, I know—you can't always tell which part of the crowd is cheering. Binky, forget it, please. Stop worrying. Doro will tell you everything you need to know."

Now, in the almost deserted corridor—the closing bell had rung, and Binky realized she was about to miss her bus —Doro said, "I'm supposed to start working with you right away, Binky, because, my gosh, it's already Tuesday, and we have a rally Friday night. . . . Come on, the first thing to do is see if Cathy's skirt will fit you. If not, we'll just have to scrounge around—maybe borrow one from the JV squad, I think Lisa Bowden's about your size. . . . What's the matter?"

"I've got homework!" Binky said. "And—and a whole bunch of other things I wanted to get done this afternoon." She looked wildly down the expanse of corridor to the doors at the far end. A gleam of yellow, a black number 12—sure enough, her bus was about to depart.

"Like what?" Doro demanded. They were all staring at her—Sue and Caroline and Heather Miles and two other girls whose names Binky didn't know, a chunky redhead and a languid-looking girl with a lot of blue-black hair and a layer of eyeshadow to match.

How could Binky tell them she'd planned to spend the afternoon hunting in the woods behind her house for an obscure fall-blooming vine known as hog peanut *(Amphicarpa bracteata)?* Not only would it sound silly, it was part of her private life and none of anybody else's business.

She was casting about for a more acceptable excuse— washing sweaters? washing her hair? washing windows?— when Sue said, "Binky, didn't Miss Walker tell you we have practice every afternoon during football season?"

Binky nodded, though she hadn't really taken in the full significance of this at the time. "Except Mondays, sometimes," she recalled aloud.

"Right," Doro said briskly. "But this happens to be Tuesday, remember? So come on, guys, time to get this show on the road." She turned and led the way back down the corridor toward the gym with her long-legged purposeful stride.

"But—"

Binky thought of explaining that she hadn't expected to begin right away, not this very day. And furthermore, that she hadn't expected this cheerleading business to be—well, quite such a big deal. But of course she couldn't say that. It would sound superior and snooty, which Binky knew a lot of people thought of her as being anyway. Besides, her bus had left. Binky wondered forlornly how she would get home.

Which reminded her . . . "I have to make a phone call first," she told Sue. "Let my mom know where I am."

"You can call from the locker room, there's a pay phone there, remember?" Sue said, hurrying her along. Binky didn't remember; she'd had enough of locker rooms during her gymnastics career, and had spent as little time as possible in this one. You were required to take two semesters of gym, but she'd gotten those over with freshman year—field hockey, modern dance, tennis—and hadn't been near the locker room since.

Sue gave her an anxious look as they pushed through the heavy swing doors. The other girls had already gone on into the changing area; Binky could hear a babble of talk and laughter beyond the partition, the harsh metallic clash of locker doors being slammed shut. She inhaled the familiar pungent locker-room smell and tried not to make a face.

But Sue noticed. "Oh, hey—you're not going to change your mind, are you, Binky? I mean, we really have lots of fun, and you get to meet some super people. Boys, for instance." Sue gave her up-and-down-the-scale giggle. "Well, I guess you go more for the intellectual type, like Spencer Bryant—I think he's neat, only he scares me, he's so smart —but some of the jocks are really nice, too."

"Spencer's just a friend," Binky said a bit grimly, unloading her schoolbooks onto one of the benches. Spencer didn't know yet what Binky had done. She had a sudden horrid feeling that instead of being impressed, Spencer was probably going to laugh his head off. If he does, Binky thought, I'll kill him.

"Even the Bumble isn't so bad, once you get to know her," Sue rattled on. "She's the assistant coach, but actually she takes most of our practices now that Miss Walker's head of the P. E. department." Mrs. Bumbry was one of the younger gym teachers, renamed Bumblebee because of a tendency to hover. "She's kind of nosy, but she means well."

"I know," Binky said. "I had her for hockey freshman year. She was always saying what a shame it was I'd had to give up gymnastics. I think she thought I'd lost my nerve, or my parents had made me stop, or something. So finally I stuck out my chest and said, 'Look!' I mean, a top-heavy gymnast . . . Actually, it affects your whole center of balance—you practically have to start learning all over again."

Sue gave a hoot of laughter. "Binky, you didn't! What did the Bumble say?"

"Nothing," Binky said, with a reminiscent grin. "She just sort of choked."

"Was that really why you gave up gymnastics?" Sue asked curiously. "I mean, you were so *good*, Binky."

"Partly. But also, if I'd gone on with it, there would've been lots of traveling and stuff, and I couldn't see putting my family through all that. The expense, too." Binky felt in her wallet for a dime. "Also, I think I was just getting bored. . . . Where's the phone, Sue?"

"Just outside the shower room."

The usual brilliant arrangement, Binky thought, remembering other locker rooms and other phones. But at least there was no one in the showers at the moment; she wouldn't have to shout.

Sue trailed after her, looking anxious again. "So I guess you're going out for cheerleading mainly for the exercise, right, Binky? Like that's one thing about us, compared to most of the other squads around here—we really get into it, you know? Not just a bunch of dumb disco steps and a sloppy pyramid once in a while. . . . Well, we do use a pyramid, of course, but it's a tight one. We go into it really sharp, and usually we come out with a tension drop into a forward roll, or sometimes a flip-out. You'll be bird, since you're light, like Cathy." Sue's voice grew wistful. "In fact, we're good enough to do really well in competition with other squads, if Miss Walker would only let us. But she says cheerleading should never be considered a sport in itself, only part of a sport, and she's not about to let us turn ourselves into a traveling circus."

Binky had no idea what Sue was talking about, but this didn't seem the moment to ask. She listened to the phone ringing at home—seven times, eight, nine. Mom must be out on a job. Finally her younger brother Dennis answered, sounding breathless. He'd probably been outside in the yard kicking his soccer ball around.

"I have to stay after school," Binky told him tersely. "For cheerleading practice. I guess I can take the late bus, but maybe Mom could meet me at the corner of Bedford and Walnut, if she's back in time. I mean, otherwise that bus takes forever, and—"

"Lynette can take you home, Binky," Sue interrupted in Binky's ear. "She got her license last week, and she lives out your way."

"No, never mind, Dennis"—Binky nodded acknowledgment at Sue; which one was Lynette?—"I guess I've got a ride."

Her voice collided with Dennis's belated squawk of astonishment. "Cheerleading? Did you say *cheerleading?*"

"Right," Binky told him. "Listen, Dennis, I've got to go."

"Binky, you've got to be out of your mind!"

"Probably," Binky agreed, hoping Sue couldn't hear Dennis's end of the conversation. "But I've already said I'd do it, and—I'll talk to you later, Dennis," she said loudly, to cover a sound like Dennis throwing up. "It's not absolutely definite yet. I mean, I can probably still change my mind."

"You'd better," Dennis said hoarsely. "My own sister—"

"Good-bye, Dennis," Binky said, and hung up. Seeing

Sue's expression, she said hastily, "I didn't really mean that. It's just—well, I guess it's going to take my brother a while to get used to the idea. He's a soccer player, and he's only a freshman, and . . . I mean, he's probably never even *seen* a cheerleader. He just thinks they're weird, that's all."

This explanation seemed a bit awkward, even to Binky; but Sue's face cleared. "Oh, sure. Soccer players. I used to date one. How would they know anything about cheerleaders? I mean, you can't have cheerleaders at a soccer game, the way the guys never stop running up and down the field except when someone gets hurt. Like when would you ever get to do your cheers?"

Binky was saved from answering by the reappearance of the other girls, carrying various articles of clothing—or rather, variously sized red pleated skirts and bulky white sweaters. They themselves had changed into shorts and T-shirts . . . identical red running shorts and white T-shirts, Binky saw with a sinking heart.

"Do we have to wear uniforms even for practice?" she asked.

"Uniforms? Oh, these. Well, of course," Caroline Horner said. "It helps us see the formations."

The tall black-haired girl snapped her gum and said laconically, "Once I showed up in a blue T-shirt, and *she* practically killed me."

She was Miss Walker, Binky gathered from Doro's next words. "Come on, everybody, into the gym—Miss Walker's waiting for us. Just leave that stuff on the bench so Binky can start trying it on. Sue, you haven't even changed yet— move it! And Lynette, if you want to live, get rid of that gum. You know how Miss Walker feels about gum."

She turned back to Binky. "Come on down to the gym as soon as you're done, okay? I hope you can find a skirt that fits—they have to be specially ordered, and there won't be time before Friday. . . . By the way, we have to provide our own practice gear. Don't worry about today, you'll just be observing. But anyway, the shorts are eight ninety-five at Bateman's. Better get a couple of pairs, and watch it when you wash them—they run. Oh, yes, and saddle shoes. You'll have to buy those yourself, too."

"Saddle shoes?" Binky echoed.

Doro was herding the other girls into the short corridor that led to the gym. "The best ones are at the Walkway," she said over her shoulder. "Thirty-two-fifty, but they'll give you a discount if you tell them you're a Cameron cheerleader." She turned away with an automatic flip of her hair. "Be sure to get the kind with rubber soles."

The gym door swung open and shut. "Saddle shoes," Binky said again, into the silence. She'd never even *seen* saddle shoes, except in old movies on TV, the kind with Mickey Rooney in them, and had supposed they were extinct, like high-button boots. Mickey Rooney also wore oversized cardigan sweaters in those movies, and carried a megaphone. Would there be megaphones, too?

With a groan Binky sank down onto the bench, shoving aside the pile of clothes.

"Did you say something, Binky?" Sue called from beyond the partition. Binky had forgotten she was there.

"No," she said, trying to compute what all this was going to cost her. A good fifty bucks, minus discount, but plus tax. And Miss Walker had said something about paying your own cleaning bills. . . . Her parents would have a fit, even though Binky would use her own money, saved from her summer job as a crafts counselor at a day camp—saved for a lot of things that had never in her wildest dreams included red running shorts (Binky never wore red) or, for heaven's sake, saddle shoes. Well, her parents would probably have a fit anyway, Binky thought. In fact, she herself was on the

verge of one, a real, honest-to-goodness, bright-red screaming fit—because what on earth had she got herself into? If it
hadn't been for Spencer Bryant, her so-called good
friend . . .

"Student apathy," Spencer had said with a yawn, ripping
his latest editorial from the typewriter and tossing it across
the desk to Binky. "I'd like a nickel for every dreary editorial on *that* subject that's appeared in the *Scroll* over the last
ten years. Of course, mine is more stylish than most," he
added modestly.

"I'm sure," Binky said, yawning herself.

"Actually, you're a good example," Spencer said, eyeing
her thoughtfully.

"I am? Of what?"

"Of student apathy, dope. The whole syndrome. Look at
you, yawning away, bored with school"—Binky wanted to
object that she'd only yawned because Spencer had, but he
was already moving into high gear—"and why? Because if
you don't give anything, you don't get anything. Or, to
quote my own immortal words, which you can have gratis,
no subscription necessary, you get out of a situation only
what you put into it. Someone like you who just goes
through the motions, who never gets involved in anything—"

That was when Binky had made her protest about the
yearbook and the variety show tickets; when Spencer
laughed and said, "Oh, come *on,* Bink. I mean, don't strain
yourself"; when Binky said she didn't notice *him* killing
himself for dear old Cameron High, and Spencer raised his
eyebrows at the cluttered newspaper office around them,
and Binky said, "Oh, Spencer, you know you do all this
stuff practically in your sleep, and besides, it's part of your
image," and Spencer retorted loftily that editing the paper
was still a big responsibility, and as for images, maybe it was

time Binky did something about her own. "Little Miss But-ter-Wouldn't-Melt-in-Her-Mouth, whatever that means exactly—anyway, Miss Above-it-All, who can't be bothered with the masses and their childish concerns, let alone *contribute* anything. . . ."

Even as Binky slammed out the door, a part of her mind knew perfectly well that it was Spencer who was bored, that he'd been needling her only for lack of anything more interesting to do before his next class, that in fact he felt a mild contempt for what he called the gung-ho types who were always putting their names on sign-up sheets. But still . . . still . . .

I might as well have signed up for the Army, Binky thought now, glumly propping her chin in her hands. Uniforms and rules and schedules and no free time ever again, and not even getting *outside;* except at the football games, of course. For a moment she thought longingly of the gold-dappled woods behind her house, of afternoon rambles with sketch pad and paintbox and her battered copy of *A Field Guide to the Wildflowers.* At the very least she'd thought cheerleading practice would mean getting some healthy exercise out in the fresh air. But even on a beautiful day like this one, it seemed they held practice in the stuffy old gym.

Resignedly, Binky reached for the pleated skirt nearest her, saw C. RUBINO on the name-tape, and stood up to hold it against her.

"Good grief!" she said aloud, just as Sue nipped around the corner in her practice clothes, heading for the gym.

"What's the matter?" Sue skidded to a halt.

"It's so *short!*"

"So? We have panties that match. Besides, Binky, you've got good legs, what're you worrying about?" Sue flashed her a grin, and was gone.

Numbly, Binky sloughed off her jeans and stepped into

the tiny skirt. It was a bit loose around the waist, but if she moved the button a half inch or so . . . Avoiding the mirror, she put on C. Rubino's sweater. It had a big red c on the back, and the name of the team, WIZARDS, on the front. (An odd name for a team, Binky had always thought; for her, it conjured up visions of elderly men in spangled cloaks and pointed caps rather than football players in shoulder pads and helmets.)

The sweater felt as much too big as the skirt felt too short. Binky turned warily toward the full-length mirror, ready to recoil from her reflection. But actually . . . actually, she didn't look too bad, Binky thought in surprise. Peculiar, and certainly not at all like herself, but not *bad.* The off-white shade of the sweater was good with her dark coloring, and its bulkiness concealed most of what Binky still considered (despite her joking words to Sue) her embarrassingly full bosom. As for the skirt—well, Binky had to admit it was kind of cute, the way the pleats twitched when she moved and then fell neatly back into place. Maybe if she thought of it as a variation on wearing shorts, she wouldn't feel quite so—well, bare. Maybe saddle shoes would even help; as it was, her small, high-arched feet in their grubby sneakers looked awfully little and far away. . . .

If only the red weren't so *red,* Binky thought—exactly the kind of loud, assertive color she normally shied away from. On the other hand, she supposed she'd better get used to asserting herself if she was going to be a cheerleader at all. The thought made her swallow. After all, you're not going to be alone out there, she reminded herself; there'll be all the other cheerleaders, to say nothing of the players. People will be watching them, not you.

So relax, Binky told herself, and cocked one hip. The red skirt gave a sassy little twitch. A matching hairband might look good, she thought; she always used to wear one when she did gymnastics, to keep her dark curls from tumbling into her face. If she could even find a hairband that particular glaring shade of red . . .

She did an experimental spread-legged leap in front of the mirror. As she came down, she struck herself on the chest with one fist and flung her other arm out horizontally, in what she imagined to be a cheerleader's pose. "Yay, team!" she yelled.

It looked okay, she decided; except that it also looked silly.

No, it does *not,* she told her reflection sternly. And you can just stop acting so arrogant about this whole thing, Binky Nolan, like you're doing everybody a big favor. "Cheerleading? Oh, sure, I can do that with one hand tied behind my back, nothing to it." Well, obviously there *is* something to it, and the sooner you begin learning it, the better.

Having concluded this lecture to herself, Binky bent to pick up her jeans and shirt from the floor where she'd dropped them. Then she straightened again, chewing her lip thoughtfully. Just observing today, am I? she thought. Uh-uh, I don't think so. In fact—no way.

She took one last look in the mirror, adjusted the sweater so that the red letters spelled WIZARDS in a straight line, and ran lightly along the corridor to the gym door. Through the eye-level window she could see Miss Walker—short gray hair, white oxford-cloth shirt, tweed skirt, white sneakers, a whistle around her neck—haranguing the cheerleaders about something while they stood in a dutiful semicircle before her. She also saw a line of padded mats running the length of the gym floor.

Binky drew a steadying breath. Then she shoved open the door, produced her widest smile, yelled, "Yay, team!" and proceeded to turn a series of perfect cartwheels from one end of the gym to the other.

2

"Okay, okay, just don't say it, Dennis," Binky warned, coming downstairs on Friday evening. *"I* think I look cute." She turned smartly at the bottom of the stairs with a flick of her little red skirt.

"Adorable."

"Come on, Dennis, you don't even go to the games," Binky said, whirling back to glare at him. "What's it to you?"

"I'm embarrassed," he said succinctly.

"But if you're not even there to see me—"

"I'm embarrassed for *you.*"

"Dennis—" Binky stared at him helplessly. The trouble was, she knew exactly how he felt. "You'll get over it," she said, and hoped this was true. "Come on, dinner must be almost ready. Mom's doing stir-fry again, but Dad's making garlic bread."

Dennis's scowl only deepened; too late, Binky remembered that he wasn't eating bread these days—or potatoes or macaroni or doughnuts or cookies, anything that might add an extra ounce to his skinny frame. He was afraid if he grew any bigger he'd lose his position as right wing on the JV soccer team. You had to be small and agile to be a good wing, he'd explained. Well, agile, anyway. Even Dennis couldn't ignore the fact that he was gaining vertical inches, if not horizontal ones; at fourteen he already towered over Binky.

"I just hope you don't end up with anorexia," Binky said worriedly. "I guess it's mostly girls that get it, but still . . . Mom!" She halted in the kitchen doorway. " 'Hot wok, cold oil,' remember? You're not supposed to put the oil in until the wok's heated up and you're ready to start cooking."

"My daughter the gourmet cook," Liz Nolan muttered, slamming down the bottle of peanut oil. "No, my daughter the cheerleader," she said as she turned from the stove. "Good grief. I mean—well, my goodness, Binky."

"Get a load of those *shoes*, will you?" Dennis said from behind Binky.

"Rosemary, my child!" With a flourish of his breadknife their father staggered back against the counter, gazing at Binky as if overcome. "Ah, the lost days of my youth—how it all comes back to me. . . . Bands playing, pennants flying, pompoms, giant chrysanthemums. . . . The roar of the crowd, the smack of the pigskin. . . ."

"Giant chrysanthemums?" Binky said.

"We used to pin them on our coats," her mother explained. "But that was just at college games, Gerry. Speaking of flowers, Binky—"

"Well, I think you look just great, kiddo," Gerald Nolan interrupted, slinging the breadknife aside and giving Binky a bear hug. "The very model of a model cheerleader. You're gonna knock 'em dead."

"Just don't put too much garlic in the bread tonight,

though, Dad, okay?" Binky said. "I don't want to burp in the middle of a cheer, or get the hiccups, or something."

"Heaven forbid," her father agreed. He went back to his breadboard after a quick, shrewd glance at Binky, as if he could see the way her stomach was churning.

Actually, Binky felt both hungry and sick at the same time, the way she used to feel before a big gymnastics meet. "Will we be eating pretty soon?" she asked her mother. "Lynette's picking me up at seven, remember."

"We'll make it," Liz assured her, hacking away at a couple of green peppers in much the same way, Binky thought, as she hacked scrap metal to slivers out in her workshop behind the garage. Liz Nolan was a real-estate photographer by trade, but her true passion was junk sculpture. "I forgot to put the rice on, but we can have the minute kind. Grab me the box, will you, Binky? And Dennis, you can set the table, please."

"I thought we were having steak tonight," Dennis grumbled, yanking mats from a drawer.

"Well, I decided there really wasn't enough to go around, so I thought if I sliced it thin and threw in some onions and peppers and bean sprouts and things . . . Yes, I know, Binky," she said, though Binky hadn't uttered a word, "when *you* cook Chinese, you start with a list a mile long and we have to make a special trip over to the fancy market in Livingston, and then it takes you hours to prepare it and us hours to eat it, inept as we still are with chopsticks. Delicious, to be sure. But right now it's *your* schedule I'm accommodating." She dumped the pepper chunks into a bowl and began slashing away at the onions.

"Mom," Binky protested.

"Oh, all right, I'm sorry. Just one of those days, that's all. I got lost trying to find a house over in Tucker Falls, and by the time I got there it was raining, so I'll have to drive all that way again on Monday to do the exteriors. . . . I'm glad to see you're wearing tights with that outfit, Binky. It's cold out, aside from the rain. What'll they do about the rally if it keeps on raining?"

"Have it outside anyway, I guess," Binky said, trying to sound cheerful at the prospect. "I mean, it takes a lot of rain to put out a monster bonfire. . . . Mom, I think there's still some gingerroot in the fridge. It may be a little dried out, but if you cut it in half and take a slice from the middle—"

"Picky, picky," her mother said, but in an amiable tone this time, and peered obediently into the vegetable compartment. "Oh, yes—this is what I wanted to ask you about, Binky. Is it yours?" She held up a small plastic bag containing a very bright red flower. "A carnation, presumably— though not as nature intended it, unless Burpee's has gone even madder than usual." Liz was a purist gardener in the same way that Binky was a purist cook.

"It's dyed," Binky told her unhappily. "Cameron red. We have to wear them in our hair tonight. I just hope the dye doesn't run, if it's still raining. Then at the end of the rally, we each throw ours to one of the football players."

Dennis groaned, clattering forks onto the table.

"How medieval," Liz observed, returning to the onions. "Like a knight wearing your colors—is that the idea?"

"Try for the quarterback, Binky," her father advised.

"I can't. He's Doro's boyfriend. The head cheerleader," Binky explained. "I guess I'll just have to take potluck."

"Speaking of pots—" Gerald looked at his wife. "Let's synchronize our watches, right, Liz? I turn the broiler on, you start stirring, and maybe everything will come out even."

"All right, but don't rush me. Now, what did I do with the bean sprouts?"

"Behind the oil," Binky said, clapping the lid on the Minute rice and looking up at the clock. She forbore to mention that when you used canned sprouts, you were supposed to soak them in ice water beforehand, to get them crisp.

"Can't have Binky gulping her food," her father said, arranging his garlic-buttered loaf on the rack. "Not if she's going to be hurling herself about all evening."

"Oh, we won't be doing much hurling tonight. Mostly just jumps and stamps and pom-pom routines. For leading the cheers," Binky explained, as everyone looked at her. Her stomach was beginning to churn again. "I just hope I can remember them all. It's been worse than memorizing poetry for Mr. Thibold in seventh-grade English. And then there's the Alma Mater we have to sing at the end." She shook her head. "I never even knew we *had* an Alma Mater before."

"You can always fake it," Gerald said comfortably. "Just keep moving your lips, no one will notice if you're half a beat behind. . . . Easy on the soy sauce this time, okay, Liz?"

"Binky doesn't fake things," Liz snapped, turning on the burner under the wok. "In spite of her Irish blood. And I've already measured the soy sauce."

"Oh-oh. Here comes your mother's hot Italian temper," Gerald teased. "Cooking Chinese always seems to bring it out, for some reason."

"If you want to *eat,*" Liz said, slamming down her wooden spoon and turning to glare at him, "shut up!"

"Mom," Binky said pleadingly. "Dad. Please. It's after six-thirty."

"Yeah," Dennis said. "And let's not get into that ethnic thing now, for Pete's sake."

Binky agreed fervently, especially because the "ethnic thing" always seemed to come back to the matter of her own name. Liz Nolan had insisted on naming her firstborn after a beloved Italian grandmother, to preserve her precious heritage. Gerald had been appalled. Bianca Nolan— what kind of crazy name was that? As for the beloved grandmother, she'd died when Liz was only two; as for ethnic heritage, Liz hadn't been raised Italian and didn't look it, either, with her smooth red-blond hair and blue eyes. (But neither, Binky thought, did she look like the kind of person who would spend her weekends poking around town dumps in search of old stovepipes and rusty sewer grates.)

Gerald had decreed that the baby would at least have a nice, traditional Irish middle name—and further, that since a lot of people went by their middle names, he would call his daughter Rosemary.

Binky figured she might have had an identity crisis by the time she was five if it hadn't been for Dennis. As a baby, he couldn't pronounce Rosemary at all, and "Binky" was as close as he could come to Bianca; the parents were forced to declare a truce. Oddly enough, though, while Dennis had his mother's hair and his father's hazel eyes, Binky herself could almost have posed for the photos in the family album taken of her great-grandmother Bianca as a girl. Take away the stiff high collar, release the pompadour into its natural loose curls, and there was Binky—the same dark eyes, the curving cheekbones and stubborn, pointed chin. . . .

I wonder what Bianca would make of me now, Binky thought wryly, sitting down at the table. Half of her felt too hot and the other half too chilly, in spite of her tights. While her parents performed their cooking chores in tense silence, Binky mentally rehearsed a couple of cheers.

> *We've got the spirit,*
> *We've got the drive,*
> *We're going to eat*
> *Old Ruskin alive!*

A lot of the cheers were quite bloodthirsty, Binky had discovered. There was one that went:

> *Push 'em to the goalposts,*
> *Stomp 'em in the mud—*
> *Mash 'em up, smash 'em up—*
> *We're out for BLOOD!*

Then you were supposed to cup your ears and yell, *"What*'re we out for?" and the crowd would yell back, "BLOOD!" even louder than before. Doro had explained that this cheer was reserved for times when the Cameron team was way ahead, to keep things from slacking off.

The phone rang, and Binky got up to answer it. "Whoever it is, tell them we're about to eat," her mother said, ladling stir-fry onto portions of Minute rice.

But before Binky could say anything, Spencer Bryant's voice drawled in her ear, "Just wanted to wish you luck tonight, Binky. Course I won't be there myself, but I've got Tom Perry covering the rally. Should make a cute story— your debut, I mean."

For a moment Binky was speechless. Then she demanded, "What about tomorrow? Is Tom 'covering' the game, too? Honestly, Spencer, it seems to me the least you could do is give me some moral support! It's all because of *you* that I have to go out there and make a fool of myself—"

"You won't," Spencer predicted calmly. "I just happen to hate football. Wild horses, and all that—you know. Sorry about that, Bink." He hung up.

Fuming, Binky went back to the table. "Sold down the

river," she said, beginning to eat rapidly and furiously, without tasting anything. "All Spencer ever cared about was a *story*. I should have known, especially the way he didn't even bat an eye when I told him about being a cheer-leader, just congratulated me on my school spirit. School spirit, ha! Spencer only edits the paper because he wants to be a big-deal journalist someday, and he only wants to be a journalist because he likes *power*. He couldn't care less about the school. He—"

"Digestion, Binky," her father said soothingly, reaching over to pat her hand. "I don't blame you for being a little nervous about this thing, but—"

"Nervous? Who's nervous?" Binky put down her fork. *"I'm* nervous," she said, and sat staring at her family. Now she could taste the soy sauce—too much, as usual; she'd be thirsty all evening. Just as well it's raining, she thought wildly.

"But Binky," her mother said, "after gymnastics—"

"That was different. For one thing, I knew what I was doing. And for another, I was just a *kid* then. Now I'm a—a private person."

"Right!" said Dennis approvingly. "Binky's just not the type to be a cheerleader," he told his parents. "I mean, take that Sue what's-her-name, remember, that used to be a friend of Binky's—"

"Streibeck," Binky supplied automatically.

"Oh, yes," Liz said. "Nice girl."

"Well, sure, she's *nice,* but, Mom, she's a flake—you know, always giggling and flirting and getting people to no-tice her. That's the way they are—cheerleaders. And Binky's not like that. I mean, at school she's quiet and sort of dignified, and she has her own thing, her painting and all, that nobody even knows about." Dennis appealed to his parents while Binky sat bemused by this brotherly portrait of herself. "So what I think Binky should do is call up Miss Walker right now, and—"

"Dennis," his father said. "You know Binky can't do that. She's made a commitment, and she's got to see it through." There was a silence. Dennis looked down at his plate. "Besides," Gerald went on, "I have a feeling Binky may surprise us all. She could turn out to be a natural at this cheerleading thing."

"Oh, great," Dennis groaned. "That's one surprise I can do without."

"You know, you could be right," Liz said, looking thoughtfully at her daughter. "I admit the whole idea has taken some getting used to, but—"

"Please, everybody!" Binky picked up her fork. "All I care about right now is getting through the rally without throwing up. And if it'll make you feel any better, Dennis, I wish I'd never even seen that dumb sign-up sheet. But Dad's right, I can't back out now. I wish I could, I've tried to convince myself I could, but I just *can't*. It comes of being a Capricorn, or something." She reached blindly for another chunk of garlic bread, thought better of it, and forced herself to swallow a mouthful of cold rice instead. "I don't want to talk about it anymore, okay? As far as you're concerned, I'm *invisible* when I put on this outfit—I'm somebody else's relative, nothing to do with any of you. So you can all just stop being tactful!"

A car horn tooted outside. Binky wiped her mouth and pushed back her chair. "Now, where's that stupid carnation?"

But before the evening was over, Binky had begun to wonder if her father could be right about her, on both counts. Once she'd gotten through the first few shivery, self-conscious minutes, she found she was actually enjoying herself, hardly aware of the rain and the chill as she pranced and stomped and exhorted in the dramatic flickering light of the bonfire. Since the weather had limited the turnout of students, the cheerleaders felt called upon to make an extra effort. And that was another thing. Binky found she *minded* the puny, halfhearted cheers that were all they could get out of the crowd at the beginning. "Come on, you guys," she heard herself yelling, "let's *hear* it for the team! With a one, two, three . . ."

"Binky, how can you keep it *up?*" Caroline Horner said hoarsely, as they took a break while the coach addressed the rally. "My throat's killing me from all the smoke, and I think I'm getting pneumonia besides."

Binky hadn't really noticed the smoke—though it was true that as the rain came down harder, the firewood crew was hard put to keep the bonfire from turning into a giant smokebomb. And she'd been jumping around so much, she felt quite warm.

"Look at her," someone else wailed. "She even has naturally curly hair!"

"Speaking of hair"—Doro Sprague was all business, as usual, even though she was shivering inside her sodden sweater—"we're gonna cut this thing short, gang, because Mary Louise has decided not to put in an appearance after all. Her special hairdo, you know."

There was a groan.

"Who's Mary Louise?" Binky asked.

"Oh, Binky! Mary Louise Capsis. You know—she's Homecoming Queen."

"Oh, yes. She's in my chemistry class, I think," Binky said. "Lots of red hair and teeth, and giggles a lot."

"Auburn, according to Mary Louise," Lynette told her. "But anyway, I don't blame her for wanting to look halfway decent tomorrow. I mean, who enjoys coming on like a hag?" She pulled at a strand of her own dark hair, which was plastered to the sides of her face. "I'm going to be up half the night just getting this mess dry," she added bitterly.

"Oh, Lynette, you can blow your hair dry for once," Sue said. "It'll look okay."

"Okay? Like a fright wig's okay? Thanks a lot."

"Well, I say let's hear it for Mary Louise and her fancy auburn hairdo," said Abby Decker, the short, chunky cheerleader whose thatch of flaming carrot-red hair no one would ever call auburn. "At least she's getting us out of here a half hour early."

Doro frowned. "Listen, I want a hundred percent from you guys for the rest of this rally—understand? So far Binky's the only one who's really been trying."

"Oh, well, it's all new to me," Binky said quickly, not wanting the others to get down on her. But no one seemed perturbed; apparently they were used to being told off by Doro whenever Miss Walker wasn't around to do it first. Tonight Miss Walker was home sensibly nursing a cold. Mrs. Bumbry had hovered for a while, and then retreated to the comparative comfort of the locker room.

Coach Myerson was winding down his speech. He, too, was asking for a hundred percent from his players and their supporters, Binky heard; also for good sportsmanship, consideration for the visiting players and *their* supporters, and a dignified departure from the field after the game was over. No fights or tearing down the goalposts, Binky took this to mean.

"So okay," Doro said, clapping her hands. "We do the Train, the Sock-it-to-'em, the Bonfire Yell, and the Snake. Watch it during the Snake, there're always a few guys on the end who try to play crack-the-whip, and with the ground so slippery, someone might get hurt. Heather, you and Caroline better bring up the rear. Sue and I will lead, and the rest of you space yourselves as evenly as you can. Got it? Oh, yes, and the flower bit. We'd better do that from up on the platform, otherwise nobody will be able to see." As the rain slackened for a moment and the bonfire flared up more brightly, Doro looked at Binky and said, "Binky, where's your carnation?"

Binky felt her wet curls. "I don't know. I'm sure it was still on a minute ago. . . ."

They all began searching for it, backing and turning, bending over to peer at their own muddy footprints. The rain sluiced down again, harder than before, threatening to extinguish the bonfire altogether, and it was hard to see. The crowd—what was left of it—was getting restless.

"Oh, well, Binky'll just have to pretend to throw something, maybe no one'll notice," Caroline said, and then stooped. "No, here it is!" She began to laugh. "Sort of."

What she handed Binky bore little resemblance to a flower of any kind—a pitiful bit of squashed red pulp, and filthy besides. Binky cleaned it off as best she could on the hem of her skirt and secured it gingerly to the bobby pin still in her hair. "Maybe I could throw it to the goalie," she said sadly. "It seems kind of appropriate."

Caroline choked. "Binky, a football team doesn't *have* a goalie!"

"Then who should I throw it to?" Binky asked.

But Caroline was laughing too hard to answer, and Doro was already lining them up for the first cheer.

Once again Binky found herself caught up in the pleasure of rhythmic sound and movement. Gymnastics was always so deathly *quiet,* she thought, and wished she could throw in a few flips, just for fun. But they were supposed to save all that kind of thing for the game tomorrow.

At the end of the snake dance, laughing and breathless, the cheerleaders wove their way up onto the platform, executed a smart shoulder-to-shoulder salute, and then unpinned the carnations from their hair. "Hey, Brett!" Doro yelled down into the group of football players, who were massed now below the platform. In their hooded scarlet raingear, their faces in shadow, they looked bulky and rather menacing, Binky thought, like extras in a horror movie. But as Doro tossed her carnation into the air, one of them stepped forward, caught it, and threw back his hood, grinning broadly. The crowd cheered. This was Brett Pastore, the quarterback, Binky gathered.

Now the other girls were pelting the team with their flowers—but not aimlessly, as Binky realized when Lynette muttered, "Oh, why does Richard have to be at the *back?* I can't throw that far. If that dumb Chuck Morris catches it, I'll just die."

Binky hesitated, saw that in another moment she would be the only one left holding a carnation—if you could still call it that—and simply flung the thing as hard as she could over the upturned heads of the players. It sailed much higher than she'd intended, and for an awful moment Binky thought no one would be able to catch it. Then a tall figure leaped into the air, stretched out a long arm, and plucked it safely down. Again the crowd cheered. "Good catch, Piers!" someone yelled.

Binky saw the tall boy examine the thing in his hand with a puzzled expression—well, she couldn't really see his face, only a thick fall of straight blond hair where his hood had slipped back, but that was the impression he gave—and had to struggle to keep her bright cheerleader's smile from turning into a fit of the giggles.

"Wow, Binky," said Sue, beside her. "Piers Anderssen! Are you serious? I mean, he's just too much."

"He is? I mean, I don't even *know* who he is," Binky explained. "I'm just glad he managed to catch my flower so it didn't look like I was just throwing it away to get rid of it."

"Well, he's a wide receiver," Sue said, obscurely to Binky. "Hey, look, I think he's staring at you, Binky, like maybe he's really interested. Oh, gosh, wouldn't that be something —you and Piers. He's new this year, a senior. . . ." She sighed.

"He's probably just wondering what happened to my poor carnation," Binky said. But as she looked, she saw the tall boy stow the sodden flower carefully in the pocket of his slicker. When he raised his head, their eyes seemed to meet for a moment over the heads of the other players.

That was all; but for a moment Binky felt slightly breathless—more so, in fact, than she had throughout the evening's exertions. Don't be ridiculous, she told herself. You're letting this whole thing get to you—bonfires and solemn coaches talking about the honor of Cameron High and our boys going out to do or die on the field of battle. As Mom said, it's practically medieval. The knight wearing my colors . . .

But before she could shake away this thought altogether, the band struck up the rather lugubrious strains of the Alma Mater, and the cheerleaders linked arms.

> *Oh, Cameron's sons and daughters*
> *Beside the Wautuck's gleaming waters. . . .*

This line had always disconcerted Binky, since most of the Wautuck River had long since been diverted to feed into a local reservoir, leaving only a sluggish brown stream that sometimes dried up entirely in the summer. As a result she missed the next line of the Alma Mater, and couldn't remember what came next.

Assuming a sincere expression, Binky mouthed some

vowel sounds, and by listening hard to Sue, managed to convert them at the last moment into words:

> *We bear the standard proud,*
> *For you our humble heads are bowed. . . .*

The bonfire flared; in its light Binky had a brief glimpse of Piers Anderssen's grave face and moving lips. She could have sworn he didn't know the words, either. But of course he was new, which gave him an excuse; which must also be why Binky had never noticed him before.

3

At halftime the score was Ruskin 14, Cameron 13.

This imbalance had come about when the place kicker, a thin, quiet boy named Ted Fiske who was in Binky's French class, missed the point after Cameron's second touchdown. Binky had been astonished to see that Ted was almost in tears as he walked back to the sidelines. She hadn't even known he was a football player; certainly he didn't look like one. But when it was explained to her that all Ted did was kick points after touchdowns—or try to—she decided he must be only a marginal kind of player. His uniform was still clean, after all, and he hadn't got himself bashed around like the others. Like Piers Anderssen, for instance, who had a raw-looking scrape on one cheek and whose white pants were streaked with mud and grass-stains. These details Binky observed when Piers left the field at the half; during the play she hadn't known which one he was.

The Cameron cheerleaders rested from their labors while the band marched around the field. Or at least they'd begun

by marching. Now they were sidestepping and backing and
turning, sometimes even breaking into a run with their instruments clutched under their arms—to the detriment,
Binky thought, of their music, which often seemed to fade
away entirely. She understood that they were forming patterns, and supposed the whole thing would make more
sense if you could view it from a seat up in the stands.

But even at bench level Binky was finding the whole
scene unexpectedly pleasing, now that all the horrible bashing and grunting had stopped for a while. Sunlight glittered
on trombones and trumpets, winked from flutes and fifes,
made a dazzle of contrast between the band's red blazers
and the rain-freshened green of the playing field. Across the
way, under a polished blue October sky, the Ruskin stands
were a blur of gold and purple. In front of them a corps of
girls wearing sequined purple bathing suits and gold cow-
boy hats shook enormous gold-and-purple pom-poms at the
people in the front rows.

("Pom-pom girls," Sue had said in disgust. "I ask you.
Who do they think they are, the Dallas Cowgirls?" Since
Binky wasn't sure who or what the Dallas Cowgirls might
be—Dallas was a big modern city, surely?—she said only,
"Well, it's a good thing they're on the sunny side of the
field. They'd freeze in those outfits over here.")

So many garish colors, Binky thought. They ought to
clash, but somehow they all went together, like the mixture
of people in the Cameron stands behind her. She hadn't
realized so many adults went to high-school football games,
nor that they brought so many little kids with them. "Always know your crowd," Miss Walker had said; and so
Binky had been studying it during the first half, in between
leaps and stomps and claps and splits and cartwheels.

It was a big crowd, since this was a homecoming game
and Ruskin a traditional rival; also because it was such a

beautiful day—"perfect football weather," as people said, a term Binky had never really understood before. Cameron students occupied the center of the stands, many of them wearing red sweaters or Windbreakers. Adults and little kids tended to sit on the lower seats to either side. Up high on the left was a bloc of giggly twelve- and thirteen-year-old girls. On the upper right a dark mass resolved itself gradually into what Doro called "the rowdy element"—a lounging group of older boys in black leather jackets who, Doro warned Binky, came to the games to jeer rather than cheer. "Usually they don't cause any real trouble, but you have to keep an eye on them. If they start yelling crude stuff, we get a big cheer going to drown them out."

In fact, much of what the cheerleaders did amounted to a form of crowd control, Binky had begun to realize during the first half—an effort to weld all these assorted groups into a unit. And when, with the other girls, she yelled, "Three, four, five, six," and the crowd roared back, "The Cameron team knows *magic* tricks!" she'd felt thrilled in spite of herself (and in spite of the fact that she'd been baffled by that particular cheer until Lynette explained, "We're the Wizards, Binky. Wizards, magic . . . see?").

But the most successful thing so far, Binky thought, smiling to herself, had been the business of the dog. Even the leather-jacket boys had cheered then.

During the second quarter a large St. Bernard had ambled out onto the field, ignoring all efforts to call it back; in fact, it seemed oblivious of its surroundings, as if it were merely taking a stroll around its own spacious backyard. Finally play had to be stopped. One of the referees made a lunge for the dog, but it gamboled heavily away from him, tossing its massive head with an air of mild annoyance, and then resumed its stately perambulation of the field.

People were laughing, but the players were getting impatient, standing around with their hands on their hips, waiting for someone to do something—especially the Cameron players, who were in the middle of a drive and had just made a first down.

Binky still didn't really understand about downs, but she did know something about momentum. So she'd run lightly out onto the field—the dog was at about the forty-yard line —and flipped a forward handspring over its broad back. The dog had stopped in its tracks, bemused. Before it could decide to move on, Binky reversed herself with a back handspring, landing neatly on its other side. Slowly the dog turned its head and regarded Binky with large, mild brown eyes; slowly its floppy tail began to brush the air. It sat down facing her, exactly as if it were saying: Hey, do that again!

Applause and cheers from the stands, whistles and cheers from the "rowdy element." "Good boy," Binky told the dog, and took a firm grip on its collar as one of the water boys came running out with a length of rope.

And the game resumed. More grunting and bashing, the smack of bone and flesh against bone and flesh—a sound Binky could hear all too clearly from her position on the sidelines. She hated everything about it. If only you could have a football game without the game itself, she thought. Even when a pass was thrown, she found herself watching not the clean, curving arc of the ball through the air but the players who were left behind, as she thought of them—the bodies sprawled on the ground, some at grotesque angles, like broken dolls. At the end of each play she prayed they would all be able to get up again.

Mostly they were and did, of course. But just before the half ended, a Ruskin player was left writhing on the grass, clutching his knee. Binky was getting used to the sight of prone figures who'd simply had the wind knocked out of them—at least she told herself she was—but a knee was something else again. She'd injured her own knee once in gymnastics practice, and remembered the terrible, sickening pain; remembered, too, how long it had been before she was able to move freely again, without fear. By the time a trainer had examined the boy and he was being helped off the field by two of his teammates, Binky was in tears.

Doro led applause from the Cameron stands for the departing player. That brought a lump to Binky's throat. "I'm glad we do that," she said to Caroline, who was next to her, and wiped at her tears with the back of her hand. Caroline stared. "Binky, for heaven's sake! If you're going to cry every time someone gets hurt—" Then she relented. "I know. But you'll get used to it. And actually, basketball is worse. You see it more close up, if you know what I mean."

While Binky was digesting this, Sue said from her other side, "Besides, you have to think of the team. *Our* team, I mean. Sure, it's too bad and all that, but that just happened to be Ruskin's best safety man. With him out of the game our wide receivers will have a better chance. Piers Anderssen, for instance," she added with a sly grin.

But Binky was still too upset to rise to this bait, or even to ask what a wide receiver was, something she'd been wanting to know.

She went through her cheerleading motions mechanically after that, and was glad when the half ended.

"It's going to be a close game, girls." Miss Walker's crisp voice aroused Binky from her reverie on the bench. She was wearing her usual tweed skirt and white sneakers, but had added a red blazer over a turtleneck sweater. Even so, she looked chilly, as if her cold was still bothering her. "I'm sure you all know how important your role will be during the second half."

They nodded dutifully.

"On the other hand"—Miss Walker's frosty gaze roved over them and settled on Binky—"I don't think we need any extra grandstanding from any of you. I've trained you as a team, and that's what I expect of you—a team effort." She stopped to blow her nose with a snowy white handkerchief.

Grandstanding? Binky knew what the term meant, of course, but in this context—

"All right, Binky." Miss Walker allowed herself a faint smile. "I'll leave it to Doro to explain to you what I mean by grandstanding. Once you understand, I'm sure there'll be no further problem."

"Well, for Pete's sake," Sue said angrily, as soon as Miss Walker was out of earshot. "When you think of how hard Binky's worked this last week—and how she came to our rescue and everything—well, she's got a lot of nerve!"

But the others were silent.

"Doro?" Binky said. "What was Miss Walker talking about? The thing with the dog? Because I wasn't trying to get attention for myself, honestly." But for an uneasy moment Binky wondered if this was entirely true. "I just wanted to get it off the field, and since nobody else seemed to be doing anything about it, I just . . ."

Her voice trailed off. Doro sighed. "I know, Binky. It was the *way* you did it."

"But I didn't even think about it," Binky protested. "Or rather, I was thinking like a cheerleader—at least, I thought I was. I mean, I figure keeping things under control includes dogs, right? So I was just trying to act in a—cheerleaderish way."

Doro said, "Well, it wasn't just the dog, Binky." She sounded uncomfortable. "I mean, I think Miss Walker is probably overreacting, what with her cold and all—and we all think it's great that you're so enthusiastic, but . . .

well, you do sort of stand out, you know. The way you're so
little and cute and athletic, besides being new. So I think
Miss Walker just wants you to tone it down some—you
know, not come on quite so strong. I know I told you to
throw in some extra cartwheels and flips and do your special things from time to time, but maybe you should save
most of that stuff for after the really big plays."

"Oh," Binky said.

"Like I could give you a signal—okay?"

"It's just so people aren't looking at *you* all the time,"
Heather Miles explained earnestly. "I mean, if they concentrate on one person more than another, it should be Doro,
because she's captain of the squad. It's nothing against you
personally, see?"

"I don't mind for myself," Doro said; and looking at her
solemn face, Binky believed her. "But it's like Miss Walker
said—we have to be a team. It's the team effort that gets the
best results from the crowd."

I got results from the crowd, Binky thought. But she
didn't say it. She felt mortified. Coming on too strong . . .
had she? But all she'd wanted was to do everything *right,*
with precision and style—to "present" herself, the way you
had to do in gymnastics if you were going to make an impression on the judges. Of course, in gymnastics you performed as an individual; even when you were part of a team,
you occupied the stage by yourself. I guess they're right, she
told herself forlornly. I'm just not used to blending in. But
besides all that . . . well, I was having fun.

And *why* were you having fun? a small voice asked her.

Oh, my gosh, Binky thought. I think I've gone power-
mad!

That intoxicating feeling, last night and again today—like
being the leader in a game of Simon Says on a grand scale.
Or like conducting an orchestra. Being able to draw the

response you wanted from a mass of people—loud, soft, fast, slow . . . playing with them; manipulating them, in fact. *That's* what I liked."

Binky sat stunned by this revelation about herself. Misunderstanding her expression, Doro gave her shoulder a reassuring squeeze, then turned and clapped her hands. "There's Miss Walker signaling—the teams are coming back. Let's get to work, you guys."

Numbly Binky joined the others to lead the roar of welcome from the Cameron stands as their players trotted back onto the field.

One result of her chastened mood was that Binky began paying more attention to the game of football. It still looked more like a war to her than a game; but she told herself humbly that if she could begin understanding the rules, she wouldn't have to depend on Doro's signals in order to avoid making a fool of herself—she'd *know* what the big plays were. But sometimes it was very confusing. When Cameron punted on fourth down, Binky was mystified by the approving roar from the Cameron stands. She jumped up into the air with the other cheerleaders, but that was all. Caroline danced over to her and said, behind her cheerleader's smile, "Binky, we didn't mean you to cool it *that* much."

"But we had to give them the ball. That's bad, isn't it?"

"Yes, but didn't you see the kick? The ball bounced out of bounds from the three-yard line. I mean, really sensational!"

Before Binky could ask why, Doro was lining them up for the "Push 'em back" yell. The players were at the end of the field farthest from Binky, and all she could see of the next play was a scuffle of red and purple.

"Which one is Piers Anderssen?" she asked Sue while the Ruskin players were taking their time in the huddle. "I mean, which end of the row is he on?"

"Oh, Binky—Piers plays *offense.*" Seeing that Binky really didn't understand, Sue relented and explained, "He's only on the field when we have the ball. You know how all the players change after a punt?" Binky nodded. "Well, that's why. It's like two different teams, see? One for offense, one for defense."

"Two different teams," Binky repeated in dismay. All she knew about offense and defense was from field hockey and soccer. "Oh, Sue, I'll never get it all straight."

"Sure you will. . . . Or maybe you can get Piers to explain it to you," Sue said with a mischievous grin.

Binky opened her mouth to say that she still hadn't even met Piers Anderssen, that she only wanted to keep track of him because she felt somehow responsible for him, as if having thrown him that poor trampled carnation might bring him bad luck. But play was beginning again—and in the next instant there was a mighty roar from both stands, soon dwindling to groans on the Ruskin side.

"Fumble!"

The Cameron crowd went wild, the cheerleaders turned somersaults, and at Doro's signal Binky obediently turned a series of back handsprings. She had a dizzy upside-down view of players trotting on and off the field. There they go again, she thought despairingly; and this time there wasn't even any punt.

Then she understood. Cameron had the ball! And they were still way down by the Ruskin goal line. "Push 'em back!" Binky yelled.

Fortunately this was heard only by Caroline Horner, who bent double with laughter as if seized by sudden stomach cramps; and as soon as Binky realized that everyone else was shouting, "Go! Go! Go!" she abandoned her own cheer (but what was wrong with it?) and joined in.

Cameron scored two plays later, and this time Ted Fiske kicked the extra point successfully.

"Way to go, Ted!" Binky called as he jogged back to the sidelines. He looked over and waved to her. She wondered if Ted felt as confused at the sight of Binky Nolan playing cheerleader as she did at Ted's appearance in a football uniform.

But the elation in the Cameron stands was short-lived. Ruskin ran the kickoff all the way back to the Cameron thirty-five, completed two quick passes, and scored. The extra point was good. Ruskin 21, Cameron 20.

"Now we'll have to start passing," Doro said, as the teams changed sides at the end of the third quarter. "I just hope Brett's wrist holds out."

"What's wrong with it?" Binky asked in alarm.

"Sprained it in practice. That's why he's hardly thrown anything except a few short passes so far—in case he had to go for the long ball in the fourth quarter."

Binky tried to imagine throwing a football when you had a sprained wrist, never mind how far. "Doesn't it *hurt?*" she said.

"Well, sure. But he's taking pain-killers, and of course he's got it taped. And the guys have been giving him great protection all afternoon. I mean, if he got sacked and happened to fall on it or something—well, that wouldn't be so good."

Binky winced. She wasn't sure exactly what "sacked" meant—it conjured up the fall of Rome in her history book —but she could imagine. Nor was she sure whether she ought to admire Brett's heroism or deplore his stupidity—to say nothing of the coach's behavior in allowing something so barbaric. The enthusiasm she'd been developing for the game, almost in spite of herself, waned. As play got under way again, she saw it once more as a lot of senseless bashing and battering. The sooner this thing is over, the better, she told herself grimly, and who cares who wins?

This mood lasted until the closing minutes of the game, when the Cameron quarterback suddenly began connecting with his receivers. Instead of agonizing over Brett's bandaged wrist and then watching anxiously each time he cocked his arm to throw, in case someone smashed him into the ground afterward, Binky found herself watching the flight of the ball breathlessly, along with everyone else.

And along with everyone else, she watched the clock. She even figured out that it stopped every time a receiver caught the ball and managed to step out of bounds. And finally, as the play came closer to Binky's position on the sidelines, she saw that the receiver over on the far side, the one who ran like a deer and who seemed to be able to pluck the ball out of the air at the last moment—sometimes catching it over his shoulder without even turning his head—was Piers Anderssen, number seventy-two.

Binky threw all her reservations to the winds—and her earlier caution, too, because surely now was no time to hold back?—and put everything she had into her cheers. But in fact there was really no need for cheerleading at this point; the Cameron stands were a solid wash of sound, with everyone standing, even the leather-jacket boys. The Cameron drive had started on its own twenty-yard line, and now, with less than a minute to play, the team was at the Ruskin thirty.

On second down, a long, long pass into the end zone . . . incomplete, the ball sailing a good two feet above the outstretched arms of the receiver (but Piers would have caught it, Binky thought). The crescendo of noise slid down the scale into groans, then leveled off again as the players went into their huddle. Binky looked anxiously at the clock and saw that it had stopped. No time to ask Sue why—the teams were lining up again.

Binky's eyes were fastened on Piers, watching him execute the curious little trot and turn she'd noticed before. The ball was snapped. Piers seemed to be drifting aimlessly at an angle toward the sidelines, a defender hovering uncertainly at his heels. Then, with a lightning swivel of his hips that left his defender flatfooted, he cut back toward the center of the field and streaked for the end zone. The pass arrowed high and straight through the air—too high again, Binky thought. But then Piers leaped. So did a Ruskin player who'd suddenly appeared beside him, but not nearly so high. There was a jar of purple jersey against red. Then Piers was rolling over and over on the ground, clutching . . . yes, clutching the football.

The Cameron stands went wild. Binky found herself jumping up and down like a little kid on a pogo stick, tears running down her face. She'd never seen anything as glorious as that leap of Piers', his body arched, his head thrown back, his arms reaching to the sky. For that moment he seemed alone on the field, a single bright figure, leaping free and exultant in a haze of golden light.

But of course he hadn't been alone; and now there was a sudden hush, as if someone had thrown a switch. Had Piers been hurt? No, he was on his feet now, still holding the ball. Binky blinked, and saw that one of the referees was making a series of elaborate gestures with his arms, that the Ruskin players were jumping up and down and clapping each other on the back, that some of the Cameron players were stomping around angrily, while others just stood with their heads hanging.

"Oh, no!" Sue groaned. "Interference. Piers must have given him an elbow, or something."

"That other player, you mean?" Binky was outraged.

"But Piers was there first. It was the other guy who bumped into *him.*"

"That's not the way the ref saw it," Sue said gloomily.

The referee had taken the ball from Piers and was marching back up the field, pacing out a long penalty.

"But that's not fair!" Binky said in anguish. "That's wrong!" She looked up at the clock, which showed fifteen seconds left to play. "Does that mean we've lost the game?"

"Time for one more play, I guess. Maybe they'll try a field goal—but I don't know, that's pretty far for Ted. . . . Come on, Binky, Doro wants a cheer."

Binky turned obediently to face the stands again, but she'd never felt less like leading a cheer in her life—except possibly the one that went "Mash 'em up, smash 'em up, we're out for *blood.*"

Cameron didn't try a field goal; instead, Brett passed again, but wildly, and the ball was intercepted by a Ruskin player, who was immediately buried under a pile of red jerseys. But it didn't matter. The gun had sounded.

People were filing silently out of the Cameron stands. Some of the cheerleaders were crying; they clustered around Doro, whose own eyes were wet, saying, "Brett tried so hard, Doro, it wasn't his fault." Doro nodded, but brushed them aside to meet the quarterback as he walked wearily off the field, his shoulders slumping. Doro put her arms around him, and Sue said, "Aw," in a tearful voice.

But Binky didn't feel like crying. On the contrary, she was seething. She noticed that the other players seemed to be keeping a deliberate distance from Piers as they milled around the benches, collecting their gear. It didn't occur to her that this might be out of respect for Piers' feelings. All she saw was Piers standing tall and apart, his helmet dangling from one big hand. His straight fair hair was darkened by sweat; his profile was expressionless.

Why, they think it's his *fault!* Binky thought in fury. Adrenaline surging, she marched over to where Piers stood, planted herself in front of him, and said, "That man needs glasses. That umpire, that whatever-you-call-him, that ref!"

Piers looked down at her, startled. For the first time she saw the color of his eyes, a clear light blue in his tanned face, like the watercolor wash Binky sometimes used when she painted a summer sky. His mouth twitched, between a grimace and a smile. He said, "Thanks, but I'm afraid he was right. It was a good call."

"Right!" Binky drew herself up, almost standing on tiptoe in her indignation. "How could he have been right? You were way up in the air before that other player even got near you. And you caught the ball! I don't see how you caught it, but you did. It was beautiful," she added fervently.

"Thanks," Piers said again, and this time he did smile a little. "But unfortunately, that doesn't matter. I was off balance when I went up for the pass," he explained, "and I got the guy with my hip. I didn't mean to, but I did. So it was a good call."

"But if you didn't mean to do it, it shouldn't count!"

"Yeah—well, it would be nice if they could call the game that way," Piers agreed. "But it wouldn't be very practical."

Binky thought about it. "I suppose not. But still . . ."

She heard a sound behind her, and turned to see Tom Perry down on one knee at the end of the nearest bench, holding a camera. Before she could say anything, Tom rose, slung the strap of the camera around his neck, gave her a wave, and sauntered away.

Had Piers noticed? Binky turned back to him anxiously, but his face showed nothing. Except that he looked tired, she realized—and realized, too, that all the other players had left the field, that Piers must be more than ready to follow them to the showers.

But she found herself saying foolishly, "Well, at least you didn't get hurt. Except for that scrape on your cheek," she added.

He touched it as though he'd forgotten about it. "Well, the ground's pretty soft," he said. "From the rain." Binky nodded. They looked at each other. "Later, when it gets cold—that's when you really feel the tackles."

"I can imagine," Binky said.

Let him go, for Pete's sake, she told herself. He must be dying for that shower, he's only standing around like this to be polite. But there was one thing more she wanted to say.

"I was afraid my carnation would bring you bad luck," she told him earnestly. "The way it was all mashed up and dirty, I mean. It fell out of my hair, and I guess someone must have stepped on it. And the way things turned out— well, maybe it did. Bring you bad luck, I mean."

Piers smiled down at her, and this time the smile crinkled the corners of his blue eyes. "I don't see how it could," he said.

"Oh. Well . . . I'm glad." In confusion, Binky turned to go. "I'll see you," she said. Then she turned back. "By the way, my name is Binky Nolan," she said in a rush.

"I know," Piers said.

Binky fled.

4

The Cameron *Scroll* came out at noon on Wednesdays. Binky grabbed a copy on her way to lunch and turned apprehensively to page two, where Spencer ran his regular personality feature, "Hallowed in These Halls." Sure enough, there was Tom Perry's story about Binky—but not just the usual two columns, she saw in dismay; instead, Binky seemed to be spread over the entire page, under the headline A SPOT OF CHEER. There were three large photographs: a head-and-shoulders closeup, a shot of Binky coming out of a cartwheel, and the St. Bernard scene—Binky down on one knee with her hand on the dog's collar, smiling what she now thought of, a bit uncomfortably, as her grandstand smile.

But at least . . . at least there was no picture of her and Piers Anderssen, Binky saw with relief. Tom must just have been using up film when he took that shot.

Then she read the article. Her relief was short-lived.

A stellar, nay a spectacular, addition to our galaxy of cheerleaders is Binky Nolan, as Cameron football fans discovered last Saturday. Of erstwhile gymnastics fame as a middle-schooler, Binky has kept a low profile since coming to Cameron.

Little did we know what we were missing! This vivacious, petite junior miss had the crowd standing on its ear, while she in turn stood on hers—or rather, while she spun and sprang and flipped from one gravity-defying position to another, in a virtuoso performance which certainly outshone the generally lackluster antics of our gallant Eleven on the playing field.

The high point of the performance came late in the first half. (Indeed, our Binky seemed a bit subdued during the second half. Could it be that other stars among the cheerleaders feared permanent eclipse?) At any rate . . .

And on into a dramatic play-by-play description of the whole silly business with the dog. Binky's cheeks burned as she read. The article seemed to go on forever, all of it written in the same deliberately overblown way. The byline might be Tom's, Binky thought bitterly, but the style was recognizably Spencer's, at least to her. And that nasty crack about the other cheerleaders . . . why, it almost sounded as if she'd *complained* about what Miss Walker had said at halftime. . . .

Binky slammed the paper under her arm and turned on her heel. Lunch could wait, or be skipped altogether; her appetite was gone, anyway. The *Scroll* office was at the opposite end of the building. Halfway down the first corridor Binky wished she'd ducked into a broom closet instead. Since Monday morning, people she didn't even know had been smiling at her and saying "Hi!" when she passed them in the halls. Now they all seemed to be standing around reading the paper. She ran a gantlet of greetings ranging from "Hey, Binky, great story!" to "How does it feel to be an instant celebrity, Binky?" This last, in a spiky-sweet voice, was from someone Binky did know, a cat-eyed girl named Melissa Grant whom Binky had always disliked.

Binky smiled, shrugged, kept going. Melissa knew (as did quite a few other people, Binky realized unhappily) that she and Spencer were friends—had been friends, she amended grimly—so of course this would look like a put-up job between them. A story for Spencer, glory for Binky . . . was that what they'd think? She gritted her teeth, turning the last corner. "Oh, look, here comes vivacious Binky Nolan," a boy sang out, falsetto, and his friend said, "Yeah, maybe that's what Piers Anderssen sees in her," and they both guffawed.

Piers? But the article hadn't said anything about her encounter with Piers after the game, Binky had been thankful to see. And she hadn't spoken to him since, only seen his tall blond head at a distance once or twice—between classes, at the back of a study hall . . .

Spencer was reading an old copy of *Smithsonian* and eating a sandwich in his favorite editorial position—chair tipped back, feet crossed on his littered desk. All he needed, Binky thought sourly, was a battered fedora to shove back on his head, and a wet cigar. He put the magazine down as soon as Binky entered. Obviously he'd been expecting her.

"Private conversation, I think," he said to a freshman girl who was going through some files in a corner. "Shut the door when you go out, will you?" The girl took a look at Binky's face and departed in haste.

"Okay, Spencer, just what are you trying to do?" Binky

slapped the newspaper down in front of him and planted her fists on her hips, glaring. "What are you setting me up for?"

"Why, Binky," he said mildly. "I thought Tom wrote a nice story about you. Everyone's enjoying it, I'm sure."

"Oh, everyone is," Binky assured him. "I'm an overnight sensation, thanks to you. As for it's being Tom who wrote that story—"

"Well, I did do a bit of a rewrite," Spencer conceded, with his blandest smile. "After all, that's part of my job. But from what Tom said, you *were* a sensation at the game. Hottest thing to hit the Cameron football field since Edgar was a pup, wherever that expression came from. I gather Mary Louise's nose was considerably out of joint. That's another curious expression, come to think of it. . . . Oh, come on, Binky," he said, as Binky stood speechless, "you remember Mary Louise. Homecoming Queen? Who sat ignored in all her finery, while all eyes were on you?"

Binky found her breath. "Spencer, that is ridiculous, and you know it. Mary Louise had her big moment at halftime, when they drove her around the field in that blue convertible with all the corny bunting. No one's *supposed* to look at her during the game. In fact what people are mainly watching *is* the game. The cheerleaders are just incidental. As you'd know if you ever went to one."

"Well, I only know what Tom reported," Spencer said with a shrug. "Course we didn't put that in about Mary Louise—she might have sued us or something. . . . Want a bite?" He held out half a sandwich.

Binky ignored it. "I've seen you do this before, Spencer," she said wrathfully. "You blow somebody up just for the fun of sticking pins in them later and watching them deflate. What've you got planned for me—a little editorial a few weeks from now, saying that a certain cheerleader seems to be overplaying her role, that maybe being an overnight celebrity has gone to her head . . . ? Something like that, anyway."

Spencer looked wounded. "Oh, come on, Binky, I wouldn't do that to you. We're old friends, remember? Besides, from what I hear, you're a terrific cheerleader, and people are going to notice you around school from now on, whatever the paper does or doesn't say. And I think that's great. You've been suppressing your true personality for too long. I mean, why hide your light under a bushel? . . . Now, there's another weird expression. I've got a copy of *Brewer's* around here somewhere—"

He twisted around to scan the crowded bookshelves behind him and added casually over his shoulder, "If I've got anything planned, it would be a follow-up interview. You know—how does Binky Nolan, a quiet, retiring type up to now, feel about her sudden emergence into the limelight. What does school spirit mean to her. Why did she—"

"Spencer," Binky said. "Lay off! I mean it." To her fury, her voice was shaking. "If you don't, I'll—I'll tell everybody about the time you plagiarized that book review for English. Oh, I know, you were just playing a game with Mrs. Gibson, betting she wouldn't recognize a *New Yorker* review if you hit her over the head with it—"

"It was from *Time,* actually," Spencer corrected her.

"Wherever. Anyway, I don't think it would sound too good, do you? Especially now you're editor of the paper."

Spencer put his feet down and propped his elbows on the desk, regarding Binky thoughtfully. He had an elfin face, with pointed ears and brown hair that grew straight down onto his forehead, and his gray-green eyes could be both merry and shrewd. His features were rather delicate for a boy, but the effect was misleading: Spencer was as tough as nails, as Binky well knew. They'd grown up together, almost literally—they'd been next door neighbors until Spen-

cer's parents got divorced and he moved with his mother to
one of the new condominiums out on Cameron Boulevard.
Binky figured she probably knew Spencer Bryant better
than anyone else did; but she sometimes wondered how well
Spencer knew her. He was like a sleight-of-hand magician,
she thought, more interested in studying his effect on other
people than in studying the people themselves.

But Spencer's next words disarmed her. "Okay," he said
quietly. "I'm sorry you're upset, Binky. I just thought if you
were going to do this cheerleading bit at all, you might as
well go the whole hog."

He paused; Binky couldn't help smiling. "I know," she
said, "another one. I think I see the *Brewer's* on the top
shelf, way over on the left."

"Well, anyway," Spencer said. "I guess the article *was*
kind of overkill. And there's one other thing. . . ." He
sighed, picked up the paper, and handed it to her. "I gather
you haven't seen it yet. Inside back page. Believe me, this
wasn't my idea, it was Tom's. He needed one more picture,
and—well, there it is."

Binky fumbled open the paper and stared, aghast. The
page was given over to candid snaps of football players and
their girls. Doro and Brett, Lynette and Richard, two other
pairs whose names Binky didn't know, and, in the lower
righthand corner, Binky and Piers Anderssen. They were
gazing earnestly into each other's eyes—as if, Binky
thought numbly, they'd been having some very private, personal, heart-to-heart conversation instead of talking about
whether or not Piers had fouled another player when he
went up for a pass. There were no captions. The page was
headed *Couples . . . and Supercouples.*

Binky sank into a chair, clutching the paper.

"I know," Spencer said uncomfortably. "I mean, I realize
you probably don't even know the guy. A jock like that—

well, not exactly your type. But Tom liked the picture, and there was a problem with the layout, and . . . well," he said again, "you know what deadlines are."

"What I know," Binky said, staring at him, "is that you're a fink, Spencer Bryant, a complete and utter fink. Piers Anderssen may be a jock, he may not have a brain in his head—I think he does, but even if he didn't—well, all I can say is, he's probably a nicer person than you'll ever be. I'm going to go find him now and . . . and apologize!"

"How do you know he's even seen the paper?" Spencer said, with an attempt at jauntiness. "Maybe he can't even read."

But Binky was already slamming out the door.

In fact, though, as she realized a moment later, halting in mid-charge, she had no idea where to look for Piers. He wasn't in any of her classes, and it was almost time for her double-period chemistry lab. After school, then. She'd hang around after cheerleading practice until the football players finished theirs, and then, when Piers came off the field—

No. In the chem lab, as Binky measured and mixed and weighted and dutifully filled in the blank spaces in her lab book, she saw that it wouldn't do. The best course was to ignore the whole thing. She was embarrassed, but so would Piers be. And if she were seen talking to him again, people would naturally assume . . . Piers himself might even assume . . .

"Oh, hell," Binky said, and spilled ammonia solution on the countertop.

Her lab partner, a quiet, studious girl named Adrienne Frank, handed her a wet paper towel and squinted at Binky through her glasses. "You okay, Binky?"

"No," Binky said. Adrienne looked at her askance. "I've got a headache," she explained quickly. "It's always so hot in here this time of day."

It occurred to her gratefully that not everybody read the *Scroll*. She herself had paid no attention to it until Spencer became editor. A serious type like Adrienne probably wasn't even aware the paper existed. After all, there were lots of Cameron students who simply went to classes and did their work and lived their real lives at home, without caring what else went on at school. Hadn't Binky been one of them herself until recently?

She was thinking nostalgically of those carefree, bygone days when Adrienne said shyly, "Are you really dating Piers Anderssen, Binky?"

Binky jumped, and spilled ammonia again. Again Adrienne handed her a paper towel, but dreamily this time. She said with a sigh, "I think he's just so beautiful. Like a Greek statue, almost." She blushed. "Sorry, I guess that sounds dumb. I mean, I don't even know him, I just know his sister, and once they gave me a ride home from school. I was only in the backseat. But still . . ." Adrienne sighed again.

Binky had opened her mouth to explain that she didn't know Piers, either, but instead found herself saying stupidly, "His sister?"

"Karen Anderssen. Haven't you met her yet?" Binky shook her head. "She's a sophomore like me, and kind of shy. At the beginning of school I helped her with her schedule and showed her around and stuff—you know. I guess it's hard being new when you're shy. Karen says Piers is shy, too, but that's kind of hard to believe, isn't it?" Adrienne stopped in confusion. "Well, I guess you'd know about that. I just meant, him being a football star and with those looks and everything. Well, anyway . . . You mean Piers never talks to you about Karen? I'd think he would."

"No," Binky said. "But listen, Adrienne, that picture in the paper—it was just a fluke, it doesn't mean anything.

Seriously. That's the only time I've ever even talked to Piers, and I'm certainly not dating him, or even thinking about it." But she could see Adrienne didn't believe her; and even to Binky her words didn't carry quite the conviction she'd intended. Who would ever have thought Adrienne Frank had such a romantic soul? Binky thought. Piers as a Greek statue . . . well, in a way, she could see what Adrienne meant.

"Why would Piers have talked to me about his sister?" she asked before she could stop herself.

But just then Mr. Vandenbusch wandered by, saying, "Enough chatter, girls," and lingered to observe their work. Binky forced herself to concentrate on the experiment at hand. After a while he observed, "You've got good, neat hands, Binky. You might consider a career in lab science someday," and wandered on without waiting for an answer.

Science? But I'm an artist, Binky thought, that's what my hands are for—and then remembered how long it had been since she'd even picked up a stick of charcoal or a paintbrush. No, I'm a cheerleader, she thought, a little wildly, with press clippings to prove it. . . .

She and Adrienne worked in silence from then on, and Binky was almost sorry when the bell rang at last, ending the school day. Time to face the public again, she thought grimly. But at least she was at the end of the building nearest the gym. She could make a beeline for the locker room and collect the rest of her gear from her hall locker after practice. . . . Then she remembered Spencer's snide remark about the other cheerleaders, and wondered unhappily what her reception would be. And there was Miss Walker to face, too. Talk about grandstanding—she could just imagine what Miss Walker would think about Binky as "A Spot of Cheer."

"About Karen," Adrienne said, as they moved toward

the door. "I just meant that she seems to be getting in with sort of a bad crowd. Mike Irwin, Bobby Gerard, older guys like that. And Cindy Brandt—she's really wild this year. It surprised me, I wouldn't have thought Karen was the type. But you know how they like to get their hooks into people, especially anyone new. I guess if you're feeling sort of lonely and out of things . . ." Adrienne shrugged, shook her head, and said, "Well, see you Friday."

Binky looked after her bemusedly. Far from being the tunnel-vision type Binky had thought her, Adrienne seemed to be a walking encyclopedia about life at Cameron High. Which just went to prove that people weren't always what they seemed. Including me, Binky thought wryly.

But she was bothered by what Adrienne had said. She didn't know Mike Irwin or the wild Cindy Brandt, but she'd been acquainted with Bobby Gerard since middle-school days—a foul-mouthed, greasy-haired boy whose mission in life seemed to be making himself as obnoxious as possible, and who hadn't improved with age. He was a senior now. Binky had noticed him in the stands on Saturday. Not exactly the company you'd choose for a shy sophomore girl who was new in town. . . . Binky shook off the thought. Karen Anderssen was none of her business, after all.

But here came someone who was—Dennis, heading for the bus with a couple of friends. Binky hailed him, meaning to tell him that if he would finish raking the leaves in their yard this afternoon, she'd take care of putting them in plastic bags when she got home. But Dennis pretended not to have heard her. He ducked his head into the collar of his jacket and went on walking. Binky saw that the tips of his ears were red, a sign that he was both angry and embarrassed. The story in the paper again. Binky could just imagine the teasing he'd taken on her behalf.

Miserably, she walked on toward the gym. Mom had told

her a few nights ago not to take Dennis' attitude too much to heart. "He's just terribly self-conscious," she'd said. "It seems to be an affliction of fourteen-year-old boys. It's not just you, it's anything that calls attention to him or makes him feel different. He wouldn't even take his lunch to school one day last week, just because I'd run out of regular brown lunch bags and had to put it in a white bag instead. I mean, imagine, a *white* lunch bag—if someone noticed, he'd be the laughingstock of the whole school. So he went hungry instead."

But Binky hadn't returned her mother's smile. She herself had never been self-conscious in that way, but she could imagine how horrible it must feel. And now, to have this flamboyant cheerleader type for a sister, her name and face and legs (she thought of the cartwheel picture) splashed all over the school paper . . .

"Hey, what's the matter?" Sue Streibeck said as Binky came dragging into the locker room. "I thought you'd be on cloud nine this afternoon."

"Oh, sure," Binky said. "Star of the cheerleading squad, which isn't supposed to *have* stars." She looked around apprehensively for the others, but saw only Lynette, absorbed in combing her hair over by the side mirror.

"Look, Sue," she said urgently, lowering her voice, "I didn't know anything about it, you've got to believe me. I mean, I knew the paper was going to do a story on me because of its being my first time as a cheerleader and all, but I never expected it to be such a big deal—all those pictures, and the kind of thing they wrote. And as for Spencer Bryant's being my friend and getting me special publicity—well, that's the last thing I'd ever want!"

It's bad enough just being a cheerleader, she almost added, but didn't, partly because she knew how ungrateful it would sound, partly because her throat had choked up suddenly and she was afraid she was going to cry.

But Sue said, "Sure, we know that, Binky."

"You do?"

"Well, of course. I mean, we knew it couldn't have been your idea—you're just not the type. Like Doro said, the paper probably needed a good story, and you're photogenic and all, so—" She shrugged.

"But what about Miss Walker? Isn't she mad at me?"

"Binky, relax! I said we understood. She knows it wasn't your fault. Anyway, she's decided it's a good thing for the team. I mean, that story ought to bring lots of people out to the game Saturday, and right now the team can use all the support they can get. And that's what really matters," Sue finished, her blue eyes round as marbles in her solemn face.

"Right," agreed Lynette, who always took in more than she seemed to, moving away from the mirror. "The good old bottom line. So don't sweat it, Binky."

The practical aspect of the thing hadn't occurred to Binky. Instead of grandstanding, it seemed, she was aiding the cause, however inadvertently. Suddenly she felt a lot more cheerful. Certainly it would be easier to put up with being a Name around school if she could think of it as serving some useful purpose. Also, it was heartening to know that her fellow cheerleaders didn't think of her as some kind of crass headline-grabber, whatever people like Melissa Grant might say. With a lighter step, Binky turned to go change into her practice clothes.

"Speaking of photogenic," Lynette drawled after her, "that was some picture of you and Piers Anderssen. I mean, wow—talk about super couples."

Binky stopped dead. "But we're not. Not *any* kind of couple, I mean. I was just talking to him about the game, that's all. I know how the picture makes it look, but—oh, for heaven's sake," she said, whirling around to glare at the other two, who were exchanging knowing grins. "I wish everyone would just stop this! He probably doesn't even know my name"—not true, she remembered a little giddily —"and couldn't care less." Which probably was true.

"That's not the impression I got," Sue said slyly, "considering that he's coming to the party on Friday. And everyone knows Piers Anderssen doesn't *go* to parties."

"Party?" But Binky had that breathless feeling again, as if someone had socked her in the solar plexus. "What party?"

"Come on, Binky, we told you about it. At Doro's, remember?"

"Well, yes, but I thought it was just if you had a guy to bring. And since I'm not dating anyone right now . . ." She stared from Sue to Lynette, and saw Lynette's blue-shadowed eyelids drop. "Hey, what is this? Did you invite Piers for *me?* Because if you did, you can just uninvite him. Of all the—"

"Take it easy, Binky," Sue said hastily. "It wasn't like that at all. I mean, he was asking Richard about you, and Richard told Lynette, and Lynette mentioned it to Doro—"

"Oh, great," Binky stormed. "And I suppose Doro just happened to mention it to Brett, and Brett, being the quarterback *and* the captain of the team, just happened to say to Piers, hey, Binky Nolan needs a date for Doro's party, you're a good team player, so how about it?"

"It wasn't like that!" Sue said again. "Doro says he's been dying to ask you out."

"Then why hasn't he?" Binky demanded. "This is the first I've heard about it. As far as I'm concerned, it's just something you guys've cooked up between you. We'd make a cute couple or something, and besides, it would be good for the squad's *image,* right? Another setup!"

She stamped into the changing area and yanked her shorts and T-shirt from her locker. The others followed. Lynette was still smiling. She said, "You really go for him, don't you?"

"So what if I do? That's my business. And anyway . . . anyway . . . What did he say to Richard about me?"

She threw out the question belligerently, challenging Lynette to make it good; but Lynette as usual was unfazed. She said languidly, "Oh, just that he thought you were cute, and were you dating anyone in particular. Stuff like that— you know."

Binky pulled her sweater over her head and said in a muffled voice, "Well, okay. But that's still not the same thing as asking me out. Which he *hasn't* done. So you can just forget about the party."

Sue sighed. "Binky, stop making such a big deal about it, will you? It's just going to be a bunch of us getting together at Doro's, and it won't even be a late party, because the football guys are in training. I mean, it's not really a dating kind of situation. Piers will just *be* there, and . . . well, so will you."

"Ha!" Binky said. "I suppose I get a ride over with Lynette and Richard, and then it just happens to work out that Piers ends up taking me home. Like that, right?"

They shrugged.

Binky glared at them for a moment, and then said, "No. If Piers is supposed to be my date, he can pick me up *and* take me home. And he can ask me first."

She pulled on her T-shirt and stepped snappily into her red shorts. Sue and Lynette turned away resignedly toward their own lockers. Binky drew in a last angry breath, and then let it out again slowly, conscious of a feeling of deflation. She remembered now what Adrienne had said about Piers being shy. He certainly didn't look it or act like it, at least on the football field—but what if Adrienne was right? Maybe he really had been getting up the nerve to call her, and . . .

Here Binky was suddenly struck by her own new image, the way she must appear to Piers—the confident, extroverted cheerleader who probably had at least a dozen boys on the string. How was he to know that except for going to the movies a couple of times with Spencer this fall, she hadn't dated anyone at all since winter, when she'd discovered that thoughtful, interesting-looking Dave Keeler in her English class was interested in only two things, (1) himself, and (2) acquiring and playing every single new video game that came on the market? And that she'd only dated two other boys—three times each—before that?

Suppose Piers was afraid she'd turn him down?

Binky perceived now that she'd been behaving in a childish way; even worse, in an unliberated way. Here were two people who simply wanted to get to know each other better, all hung up over a silly question of boy-girl etiquette. It was the kind of thing that drove Binky wild when she saw it in operation among her friends. "So why don't you just call him?" she'd often said in exasperation, when someone was languishing over a prom invitation or just a Saturday-night date that still hadn't quite jelled.

"Okay," she said to herself. "If Piers won't call me, I'll call *him.*"

She'd spoken more loudly than she realized. Sue and Lynette turned startled faces toward her, then grinned at each other. Doro, striding around the partition at that moment, slowed her steps and looked at Binky with interest. Binky could feel herself blushing, something she almost never did.

But all Doro said was "Good thinking." She gave Binky a brisk nod and surveyed the room with narrowed eyes.

"Where is everybody? My gosh, we can't afford to slack off just because it's the middle of the week. Abby? Heather? Come on, let's get this show on the road!"

Binky waited until Dennis had gone to bed to call Piers. It seemed like a long wait, what with Dennis barely speaking to her and her parents reading and analyzing the feature on Binky in the *Scroll,* in a detached manner that Binky found maddening. "Spencer's really very talented, isn't he?" her mother said. "Yes, he has a nice touch," agreed her father, who was a writer of sorts—he did promotion for a software firm. "The whole piece is facetious, of course, but done in such a way that the average reader probably won't recognize it . . . a nice little parody of the gee-whiz school of journalism."

Binky opened her mouth to point out that it was she, their only daughter, who was the subject—the victim, in fact—of this literary exercise, but closed it again. Instead, she offered to do the dinner dishes, which at least had the effect of separating her from her parents, who settled down to watch TV in the den. There was a particularly nasty stewpot to be scrubbed and soaked and scrubbed again (her mother had let the stew boil over while arguing with her father about his weekend plans—he wanted to go hang-gliding again), but Binky was glad of the exertion. The more she avoided thinking about that phone call, she'd begun to realize, the more likely she was to make it.

Even so, she found herself faltering at the last moment. She'd closed the kitchen door and got the number from directory assistance (yes, a new listing for an Anderssen with two s's, Harold); but her finger hesitated over the dial. Behind her on the table lay the much-discussed copy of the *Scroll.* Feeling furtive, as if someone might be watching her, Binky opened it to the inside back page, where tall, blond, rugged Piers Anderssen stood framed with small, dark Binky Nolan. A classic shot: the towering football player in his shoulder pads, the cute little cheerleader in her over-sized sweater. Pure corn, in fact, Binky thought, even while she examined the picture more closely. They were both in profile. Piers' head was inclined gravely toward Binky; her own was lifted to meet his gaze. And yes, there *was* something about the way he was looking at her (something, too, about the way she was looking at him). . . .

Binky dialed. A masculine voice that was not Piers' answered—Anderssen, Harold, she presumed. It was a jovial, backslapping sort of voice, the kind Binky thought of as a beer-and-pretzels voice. Except there was a slight accent, Scandinavian, Binky supposed, so pretzels wouldn't be right; herring, maybe?

She was still distracting herself with this thought when Piers came on the line. His "hello" was toneless in comparison to his father's, and his voice was deeper than Binky had remembered.

"Hello, Piers?" she said brightly. (Just *do* it, she was telling herself, ignoring panic.) "This is Binky Nolan. I met you at the game on Saturday, remember?"

"I remember."

No expression in his voice; no trace of a smile that Binky could hear. Oh, help, she thought, but plunged on with what she'd planned to say. "I hear you're going to Doro's party on Friday. Doro Sprague's," she added a little wildly, in case somehow she'd gotten the whole thing wrong. "Well, the thing is, so am I, only I don't have a date, and so I thought if you didn't have a date either, we could go together."

There—she'd said it. Her cheeks were flaming, but Piers couldn't see that.

After what seemed like a whole night and a day, Piers

said, "Sure. I'd like that." But he didn't sound as if he really meant it. Was he always like this on the phone, Binky wondered unhappily, or was it just her? Maybe girls were always calling him up this way, brazen types who couldn't wait to be asked . . . ? But if so, she told herself stoutly, he must have learned to say no. And he hadn't. He'd said, "I'd like that."

"So would I," she heard herself saying, still in that bright social tone. "I mean, it sounds like a fun party." Fun party! Binky cringed at herself; never in her life had she used that expression before. "I think it starts at seven," she babbled on. "Doro's making spaghetti, and there'll be salad and stuff." She made herself stop.

"Salad," Piers said, as the pause lengthened. He sounded bemused, as if maybe Binky thought he was a vegetarian or something. But that was better than no expression at all, Binky told herself.

"Do you want to pick me up, or—or shall I meet you somewhere?" she asked—idiotically, because where on earth would she meet him? On a street corner? In front of the all-night launderette?

"Oh, I'll pick you up. About quarter to seven—is that all right?" It was the longest speech he'd made.

"Fine," Binky said, and told him where she lived and how to get there. She spoke rapidly, to get the whole thing over with as soon as possible so that she could hang up and start banging her head against the wall. It occurred to her that now she sounded like some kind of recorded announcement relaying a set of impersonal facts. ". . . If you get to Cameron Boulevard, you'll know you've gone too far," she finished crisply. "We're south of there."

"I'm sure I'll find it okay," Piers said. Another pause. Binky was gripping the receiver so hard, she wouldn't have been surprised to feel it crumple in her hand. It occurred to her for a giddy moment that maybe Piers was doing the same thing. But no, she told herself, he just can't figure out how to end this embarrassing conversation, either.

Then he said, "I'm really glad you called, Binky."

"You are? Well . . . well, so am I." Binky gaped into the phone. "I almost didn't," she said. "Call, I mean. I was afraid you'd think . . ." Well, think what? That she was chasing him? Binky got a grip on herself. "It just seemed like the sensible thing to do," she explained with dignity. "Seeing that we're both going to the party and all."

"Sure. Good idea," Piers agreed. Then, with an effect of having cleared his throat: "Well—see you Friday, then."

"Right," Binky said briskly. "See you then."

She hung up, annoyed to find that her hands were wet with perspiration. She felt exhausted, as if she'd just finished a two-hour exam instead of a two-minute phone call. But she was also beginning to feel a bit nettled. So maybe Piers was shy—he could at least have been more . . . more *giving* over the phone. He could have said that he'd been thinking of calling her, even if it wasn't true. He—

Oh, stop thinking about him! Binky commanded herself irritably. Spencer's probably right, he's just a dumb jock, even if he does look like a—here she rejected Adrienne's Greek statue—a Viking, or a White-Russian prince, or something. I'm a sucker for good looks, she told herself, that's all it is. I would never have gotten involved with that creep Dave Keeler if it hadn't been for the romantic way that lock of hair fell down over his forehead and those deep-set eyes that made him look so sensitive and poetic. (Of course, we were reading Keats at the time.) And before that, Matt Terhune, who looked like a young John Wayne but whose idea of adventure was going to a drive-in movie—an adventure for Binky, too, as it turned out, but not the kind she welcomed. His squint had nothing to do with Western skies; he had astigmatism and was too vain to wear glasses.

Binky crumpled up the *Scroll,* tossed it into the wastebasket, snapped off the kitchen light, and turned to go upstairs. Then she turned the light back on, retrieved the paper from the basket, stuck it under her arm, and went on up to bed. This time she forgot the light, and was lectured in the morning by her father about the civic duty to conserve power, to say nothing of the high cost of electricity.

5

A few minutes before Piers was due to arrive on Friday evening, Liz Nolan remembered she was still wearing her sculptor's apron and returned it to its hook by the back door. It was no ordinary apron; Liz had cobbled it together from odd bits of leather and an astronaut's-cloth tarp which Dennis had once used on a camping trip, adding several large striped pockets made from clothespin bags—useful for holding files and chisels and tubes of epoxy.

"No point in looking too weird," she told Binky, reappearing in tailored blouse and tweed skirt. "You might as well begin by letting him think you come from a nice, normal family. Now if I can just keep your father off the subject of hang-gliding . . ."

"The boy's an athlete," Gerald objected. "He might be interested."

"These stunts of yours have nothing to do with athletics," Liz said coldly. "They're a neurotic obsession with speed and danger—trying to see how close you can come to getting yourself killed without actually doing so. One miss, and I'll be a widow with two kids to support and put through college, as I believe I've reminded you before."

"I've got plenty of life insurance," Gerald said, with a wink at Binky. "You might even be better off without me."

"Only because the insurance company has no idea of what you get up to on weekends. All they see is Corporation Man." In fact, Binky thought, her father was looking his most conservative tonight, in a dark three-piece suit. Only the glint in his hazel eyes gave a clue to what her mother called the Wild Irishman lurking inside.

Dennis slouched through the living room as the doorbell rang. "You gonna tell Piers about your wildflowers, Binky? And your fancy recipes? Or maybe you could talk about all the good books you've been reading lately—like the ones by that Wolf lady you're so crazy about." Binky had recently discovered the novels of Virginia Woolf, whose writing seemed to her almost like painting. "But no, better stick to football. That way neither of you will have to strain your tiny brain cells."

"Don't mind him, Binky," her mother said lightly, as Binky started for the door. "He's just jealous because he's still so normal. No double life, like the rest of us."

(Binky could have told her she was wrong—that a few weeks ago she'd come upon Dennis declaiming "To be or not to be" in front of his mirror in passable Shakespearean accents. She'd sneaked by his door, not wanting him to know she'd seen him, but had been impressed to realize he'd memorized the whole speech. Knowing Dennis' singlemind-edness, she figured fencing lessons weren't far down the road.)

She opened the door and had to back up a step in order to see Piers' face; she'd forgotten how tall he was. He was dressed in new-looking brown cords and a heather-brown sweater over a yellow shirt several shades darker than his hair. At least he wasn't wearing blue to match his eyes, Binky thought, a bit light-headedly; that would have been almost too much.

"Hi," she said, with her biggest smile—the smile she always seemed to produce when she felt nervous. "Come on in and meet my parents while I get the bread." Two loaves of garlic bread were Binky's contribution to the party. She'd used her father's recipe, but had also added some chopped dill.

She made the introductions hastily and went to the kitchen to take the foil-wrapped packages from the fridge, also to check her appearance in the mirror by the back door. She was wearing a new green-plaid skirt that matched her last-year's green blazer, and a white blouse with ruffles —the latest style. (Binky wasn't sure it was really *her* style, but at least all the ruffles made her look less bosomy.) She bared her teeth to check for matching bits of spinach—she'd sneaked a bite of the frozen quiche her mother had heated up for supper—and then went back into the living room.

". . . From Minnesota," Piers was saying. "That's where my dad's family comes from. But my mom's from the East originally, so when Dad was offered the new dealership here . . ." He shrugged.

"It must have been hard, moving just before your senior year," Liz said sympathetically. "But at least the winters will be easier here."

"Oh, I kind of like the cold weather," Piers said, and grinned unexpectedly. "When it's thirty below in the morning—well, that sort of wakes you up, if you know what I mean. And there's lots of stuff you can do outside when everything gets frozen really solid."

"I suppose so," Liz agreed, rather faintly. Binky saw her shoot a look at her father, in case he started asking ques-

tions about ice-boating conditions—ice-boating was a new
interest of his—on Lake Huron or Superior or whichever of
the Great Lakes Piers might have lived near. "Well, I guess
you two had better get going," she said, turning toward the
hall.

"Nice to have met you, sir," Piers said to Gerald, who
dutifully wished him luck in tomorrow's game. While this
exchange was taking place, Liz leaned close to Binky and
whispered "Wow!" in her ear. Binky frowned at her and
reached for the doorknob just as Piers' hand closed over it.
She withdrew hers hastily. Piers opened the door and stood
back to let her precede him down the walk.

But now it was Binky's turn to say "Wow!" She stared at
the car drawn up at the curb. "Is this what you usually
drive?" she said incredulously. It was a silver Lincoln with,
as Binky discovered when Piers opened the door for her,
sky-blue velvet upholstery and dashboard fittings that could
have been (were, for all she knew) made of pure platinum.

"One of my Dad's," Piers said briefly, going around to
the driver's side. Clutching her loaves of garlic bread, Binky
settled gingerly into the enveloping blue plush. *One* of his
Dad's? What had she gotten involved with, some kind of
millionaire? But then she remembered the word "dealership," and also the big new Lincoln-Mercury showroom
halfway between Cameron and the larger town of Livingston to the west.

Piers confirmed this guess as he slung his long body into
the car and started it off with a barely audible purr. "He
likes me to give the demos a spin once in a while," he said.

Demos? Oh—demonstration cars. After a pause which
Piers didn't seem inclined to fill, Binky said, "To keep them
in condition, I guess?"

"More for advertising," Piers said tonelessly, in a way
that seemed to close the subject. Binky wondered if Piers

wouldn't feel more comfortable driving the kind of much repainted and repaired heap the other boys drove; or a sports car, anyway. He must feel kind of conspicuous behind the wheel of a custom-made job like this one, designed for Arab tycoons and such. But maybe not. She could tell nothing from his expression.

They drove several blocks in silence, and Binky found herself wishing the car itself would make more noise. She'd been heartened by the easy way Piers had seemed to make conversation with her parents. Now she wondered what on earth the two of them were going to talk about for a whole evening. Or not a whole evening, she reminded herself; after all, there'd be the other people at the party to talk to. It was only a matter of getting through the drive to Doro's and then, later, the drive home. Maybe Dennis was right, she thought resignedly, and searched her mind for a question about football.

"What do they mean by a safety?" she said, just as Piers said, "What's that smell?"

"Smell?" Binky herself was conscious of inhaling only the new-upholstery smell of the car, a smell, actually, that made her feel a bit queasy. "Oh—the garlic, probably." She shifted the foil-wrapped packages in her lap, hoping she wasn't getting grease on her new skirt.

Piers rolled down his window an inch or two—or rather, pressed a button that slid it down. Binky wondered whether he was afraid the smell would get into the custom upholstery, or whether he just didn't like garlic. But she didn't ask. Instead she repeated her football question. Piers addressed himself to it seriously.

"Do you mean the score, like when you get trapped in your own end zone—that's called a safety—or the type of player?"

"I don't know. Well, both, I guess, if there are two kinds.

I've never been a cheerleader before," Binky explained, "and I hardly know anything about football. Miss Walker said I should just watch the other girls, but that's not always too easy, and besides—well, I'd like to understand what everyone's talking about, instead of its being like a foreign language, almost."

This had the desired effect, or so Binky told herself. Piers seemed only too happy to oblige with a whole glossary of football terms, more than Binky had realized even existed. But at least he was talking, and she was able to relax. She'd been partly sincere in her request, and she did do her best to listen, asking dutiful questions whenever Piers paused in his discourse. But she kept being distracted by glimpses of his profile whenever they passed under a streetlight. She could still see the scrape on his right cheekbone. She came back to full attention only when Piers described the safety (the player kind) he'd be going against in tomorrow's game against Wallace Tech.

"I guess he's pretty good—he made All-State last year as a junior. They say he plays rough and hardly ever gets called on it." Remembering what rough could mean on the football field, Binky shuddered. "If I can get him to foul me early in the game in a way the ref can't ignore . . ." He shrugged. "Well, it could open things up some."

Binky wondered apprehensively just what this might involve for Piers—letting the other player smash him to the ground and stomp on him or kick him in the ribs? Worse? But Piers had returned to his role of instructor. "Now, about third-down options . . ."

Several plays later Piers slowed to check a street sign, swung the car around the corner, and nosed it between a pair of ornamental iron gates onto a graveled driveway that swept around in a circle before a huge, white-columned house blazing with lights that looked to Binky like Tara before the Civil War—or perhaps afterward, with plenty of Rhett Butler's money in it.

She stared, and was glad to see that Piers was staring, too. "Is this *Doro's?*" she said as he braked to a halt.

Piers pulled a slip of paper from his pocket, checked the address, and said, "I guess so." He shook his head, looking at the house. "You did say spaghetti?"

"I know. It looks more like pheasant-under-glass, doesn't it?" Binky said, smiling at him; it was the first glimmer of humor he'd shown since his remark to her parents about the Minnesota winters.

Piers parked the car behind several others—normal, beat-up high-school-kid cars, Binky noticed, which must mean they'd come to the right place. As they got out, she said, "Well, at least the Lincoln looks right at home here," and added with a laugh, "Who knows, maybe they'll buy it."

Not funny, she deduced, from the way Piers stiffened up again. She gave a mental shrug, and turned her attention to the house. She hadn't had any particular picture of where Doro lived, assuming that it would be an ordinary kind of house like her own. This seemed a wildly improbable setting for tough, practical Doro Sprague. . . . But maybe she was different at home, Binky thought; maybe Doro would come to the door in some trailing garment—chiffon was what the atmosphere seemed to call for—with her hair done up in a French twist and pearls at her ears. . . .

But of course she wasn't, and didn't. Doro was dressed in jeans and a striped shirt, and she greeted them by saying briskly, "Hi, you guys. Let's see, everyone's here now except Abby and Tuck. C'mon, Binky, let's put your bread in the oven."

As she led the way past a graceful sweep of white-railed staircase and down a wide, carpeted hallway, she called, "Mom, will you answer the door? Only two more to come," and Binky had a glimpse into an enormous, richly furnished living room—drawing room?—in which two small, elderly-looking people sat reading newspapers. They didn't seem to go with the house any more than Doro did. Or with Doro herself, for that matter.

Binky felt as if she were walking through a stage set until, after several turns of the hallway—there was actually a music room with a harp in it; was it possible that Doro played the *harp?*—they came to the kitchen. It was the kitchen of Binky's dreams: restaurant-sized stove, rotisserie, butcher-block counters, a slab of marble for rolling out pastry, copper pots gleaming against the walls, strings of onions and peppers and garlic hanging from the ceiling. . . . There was even an open fireplace, with a Dutch oven for baking.

"My mom's a cooking freak," Doro said, misinterpreting Binky's expression. "She had this copied from some French kitchen in a magazine. Wild, huh?"

She slid Binky's loaves into one of the ovens and turned a burner on under a large pot of water which presumably was for the spaghetti. Next to it simmered a pot of spaghetti sauce.

"Smells good," Piers said politely.

It smells like a mix, Binky thought, and decided Mrs. Sprague could have had nothing to do with it. She also saw that the oven setting was much too high, given the length of time it would take that pot of water to boil, and managed to turn it down surreptitiously while Doro was giving a perfunctory stir to the sauce with a wooden spoon. Later she'd come back and turn up the heat again and fold back the foil so the bread would get brown and glazed and crispy on top. Maybe she could add a few herbs and spices to the sauce while she was at it. . . .

She felt Piers' eyes on her, and saw that he was watching her curiously, with a little quirk at the corners of his mouth that wasn't quite a smile. She wondered what he'd say if she told him that her idea of a really good time would be to roll up her sleeves and spend the rest of the evening in this glorious kitchen. But someone who didn't even like the smell of garlic undoubtedly knew nothing about cooking—or about good food, for that matter—and wouldn't care less.

"Okay," Doro said, handing Piers a bag of potato chips and Binky a bowl of dip, and grabbing a couple of large-size Coke bottles from the fridge, "Let's go join the party."

Despite the size of the house Binky had been wondering where the party could be taking place, since it certainly hadn't been in any of the large rooms they'd passed. Now Doro led them through a door at the end of the kitchen and up a narrow flight of uncarpeted stairs. There was another door at the top which Doro opened onto a blast of rock music.

Binky supposed you could call it a suite—but really, she saw after a moment, they were in what must once have been the servants' quarters, a series of boxlike little rooms and one larger room where the party was. There were straw mats and posters and beanbag chairs and lamps made out of bottles. It all looked a good deal more like Doro than the rest of the house.

"This is where I hang out," Doro said, unnecessarily, and Piers grinned at Binky behind her back.

Binky thought, not for the first time, how that grin transformed his face, with its almost too-symmetrical features and rather solemn expression. Now she noticed that one of his very white front teeth was slightly crooked. This discovery warmed her, somehow; so did the small flash of communication between them. For a moment she was able to forget how much she loathed loud rock music and small rooms where someone was smoking—Caroline's boyfriend, Roger, this turned out to be, his teeth clenched on the stem of a battered-looking pipe. He was a freshman at Harvard, Binky knew, and probably thought it suited his image.

She and Piers squeezed onto a small sofa next to Lynette and Richard, a maneuver made possible only by the fact that the other two were rather closely entwined. Except for Roger, all the boys were football players, and the room seemed oppressively crowded even before Abby arrived with Tuck Zeller a moment later. But at least Abby said "Phew!" as she came in, and went straight over to a window to let in some fresh air. Piers looked relieved, too; in fact, Binky had noticed a faint sheen of perspiration on his face, though the room wasn't particularly hot.

Because of the music, general conversation wasn't possible unless you shouted, so Binky tried to get a four-way conversation going with Lynette and Richard. This wasn't easy: Richard seemed almost asleep, and Lynette was in one of her more languid moods, mechanically snapping her gum while she ran her long fingernails through Richard's hair—spiky-looking brown hair which Binky couldn't imagine wanting to touch. Piers' hair was something else again, so thick and shining. . . . The whole side of Binky's body felt tingly where it unavoidably touched his, crowded together as they were on the sofa. Piers had adopted a lounging position, his hands in his pockets and his long legs stuck out straight in front of him and crossed at the ankles; but Binky could feel he wasn't any more relaxed than she was.

"This is some house," she said to Lynette. "Does Doro have any brothers or sisters? I mean, it's so big." And empty, she almost added.

"Nope. Well, not as far as she knows, anyway. She's adopted."

"Oh," Binky digested this. "What does her father—Mr. Sprague, I mean—do?"

"Do?"

"For a living," Binky said impatiently. Sometimes Lynette was really too much. "They must have a lot of money, to live like this."

"Yeah, I guess. Let's see—I think he invented something." Lynette frowned in thought. "Some little gadget to do with rockets, maybe? Something like that. Anyway, they only moved in here last summer. Doro hates it. Not her scene, you know?"

Binky turned to Piers, but he didn't seem to be listening; he was staring at his shoetips. Or maybe he was listening to the horrible music, she thought. So much for flashes of communication. It began to look like a very long evening.

But just then Abby and her boyfriend, Tuck, came over to the driftwood table in front of the sofa to help themselves to onion dip and stayed to talk, and things improved. Binky liked Tuck, who had an engaging grin and a quick sense of humor. He was also not a football player, a fact that appealed to Binky at the moment; his sport was ice hockey. Tuck was chunkily built, with flaming red hair that was almost the same color as Abby's. In fact, he and Abby could almost have been brother and sister, Binky thought, and found herself envying the way they seemed to be so totally at ease with each other. Opposites might attract, she reflected, with another glance at Piers' profile, but what did they do after that?

It seemed that Tuck knew Piers from a couple of classes at school, and he soon had Piers drawn into the conversation—or at least had Piers responding with more than polite monosyllables. And when Tuck said, "Hey, I hear they've already got snow up in Vermont," Piers' eyes brightened, he abandoned his slouch and leaned forward with what, in Piers, amounted to positive animation.

"Course it won't be anything like what you're used to back home," Tuck said, "even if it's a good year. We measure snow here in inches, not feet. Heck, fractions of inches sometimes. Still, it's enough to slap your skis onto, and like they say, the boulders you can't see won't hurt you." He grinned. "It's just the others you want to watch out for."

It turned out that Abby, too, was an avid skier, and for a while the three of them discussed various experiences they'd had, argued the merits of different kinds of equipment, compared open slopes with trails, talked weather conditions and types of snow. . . . Binky half listened, watching Piers— the way his big square hands gestured as he talked, the habit he had of chewing his lower lip and nodding vigorously when someone said something that interested him. He wasn't like this when he talked about football, she thought. But maybe that was only because with her it was such a one-sided conversation.

She imagined Piers on skis. She saw him hurtling down a steep white slope, leaning and twisting the way he did on the football field, then crouching over his skis to shoot like an arrow for the finish line, swift and fearless. He would be wearing a light-blue windshirt that matched his eyes, his face would be intent and glowing . . .

She felt someone watching her, and saw Sue Streibeck grinning at her from across the room in a way that said, You've got it bad, kid. Binky frowned, consciously wiping away whatever dumb expression she'd had on her face, just as Piers turned his head, looked at her with shining, serious blue eyes, and said, "Do you ski, Binky?"

Binky felt as if she were in an elevator which had suddenly dropped four floors. In fact, it was not unlike the feeling she got whenever she found herself at the top of a high hill, a high building, a high anything—except right now it was all mixed up, too, with the way Piers was looking at her.

"I've done some cross-country," she said lamely. (Twice to be accurate, and had found it very tedious.)

Tuck gave a snort. "Oh, well, sure—the in thing. How to work up a sweat and die of boredom while slowly going nowhere for hours on end."

"I meant downhill," Piers said.

Binky looked away from his intent gaze. "I've never really been into skiing," she said with a shrug.

Abby said enthusiastically, "But you're such a good athlete, Binky. I bet all you need is a few lessons. I should think you'd be a fabulous skier."

"I—I don't like the cold," Binky said, and then, as the light went out of Piers' face, added hastily, "I mean, I don't mind cold weather in itself, it's just that I got really frostbitten when I was a little kid, and three of my toes still turn white whenever my feet get cold."

This was true enough; and the adventure which had caused it—a snowshoeing expedition with her father into the woods behind the house in what had turned into a howling blizzard, so that they'd had all they could do to make it back to their own kitchen door—made a funny story (not that it had seemed so funny at the time). Binky found herself telling it now as if she had nothing more on her mind than being the life of the party. Abby and Tuck laughed, and Piers smiled politely, but she could feel that he had withdrawn into himself again.

Of course, the real truth had nothing to do with frostbitten toes. Binky would willingly have frozen all ten toes and all ten fingers in exchange for the ordinary person's capacity to enjoy being at the top of a mountain (or an observation platform, a Ferris wheel, even the top balcony of a theater) without seeing specks in front of their eyes and feeling sick and faint, on the black verge of pitching down forever into space. . . .

Fear of heights: acrophobia. But knowing the name for it, knowing that many otherwise normal people suffered from it, too, didn't make Binky feel any less ashamed of her fear. In fact, even within her own family she'd managed to conceal the extent of it from everyone but her father, who'd tried to help but had only made things worse, and who'd ended by consoling her that the fear would probably recede as she grew older. Maybe; but Binky wasn't eager to put that to the test. Instead, she'd learned to avoid situations which could reduce her to what she thought of as a disgusting, gutless blob of cowardly jelly. Downhill skiing, for one.

But she wasn't about to explain that to anyone.

Suddenly all Binky wanted was to escape for a few minutes to the sanctuary of the kitchen. Time to tend to her garlic bread, anyway, and maybe sneak some oregano into the spaghetti sauce—a little tomato paste, too, if it still hadn't thickened up properly. . . . But she was too late. Doro and Heather Miles were sticking their heads through the door, yelling, "Come and get it!" and in a moment they were all trooping downstairs.

Binky had wondered where they would eat, since the kitchen table wasn't big enough for them all, and the formal dining room she'd seen in passing looked as if it were reserved for five-course dinners, with candelabra. But it turned out there was a breakfast room off the kitchen, all done up in yellow gingham and blue crockery, and that was where Doro had laid out the food, on a big round table covered with a gingham cloth.

The spaghetti was soggy, the sauce tasted exactly as Binky had expected it to, and her own garlic bread was still damp on the inside, with nothing you could call a crust. But Heather had made a good green salad—and at least, Binky thought, they'd gotten away from the music. Also, they were no longer arranged in pairs, like animals in the Ark. It was a relief to have Piers across the table from her, where she could enjoy looking at him without having to try to talk to him.

Roger, the Harvard freshman, was on Binky's right, his pipe mercifully set aside for the moment. Winding spaghetti on his fork, he said, "Where'd you get a name like Binky?"

Disliking his tone, Binky said a bit stiffly, "My real name's Bianca."

"Italian, huh?" He scrutinized her for a moment, and then shook his head. "Nope. Bianca doesn't suit you at all. Too romantic, or something. Binky's good, though—a cute cheerleader-type name."

Stung, Binky said, "I haven't always been a cheerleader, you know."

"That's right, Caroline said you were new to the squad, or the team, or whatever it's called." He sighed. "I can't imagine how *she* got mixed up in this cheerleading business —not her kind of thing at all, I wouldn't think. But I suppose there are all kinds of peer pressures in public school. I went to prep," he added unnecessarily.

Binky suppressed an impulse to dump her plate of spaghetti into Roger's gray-flannel lap. She said coolly, "Well, *I* can't imagine Caroline's doing anything she didn't want to do, and never mind peer pressures. We don't just go out and wave pom-poms around, you know. Cheerleading takes athletic ability, and a lot of discipline and practice, at least the way we do it." Hey, listen to me! she thought in some amazement.

Roger looked unimpressed. "Well, luckily Caroline's a bright girl," he said judiciously. "She shouldn't have any trouble getting into one of the top colleges. I suppose she can afford to spend the time."

The implication being that all the rest of them were featherbrains whose time was of no importance. Seething, Binky

managed to say in her most noncommittal voice, "I'm plan-
ning on Stanford, myself"—only because she'd heard Stanford was even harder to get into these days than Harvard.
Actually, she was looking for a small liberal arts school
with a good fine-arts department, and prestige was the least
of her concerns.

Roger was regarding her with a mixture of skepticism
and uncertainty that Binky would have found comical if she
hadn't been so incensed. Before he could ask her what her
PSAT scores had been—quite good, as a matter of fact, in
the verbal and so-so in the math—Binky turned to Sue on
her left and complimented her, in what she hoped was a
suitably frivolous, cheerleader-type way, on her new short
haircut. Sue obliged with a detailed account of her session
with the hairdresser, and went on to relate what her mother
had said about it, what her best friend, Janet, had said, and
what her date for the evening, Alan, had said: "I liked it
better the other way."

Alan, a big beefy senior who played tackle (or was it
guard?) might have had no imagination when it came to
hairstyles, but he took his football seriously. When he
pushed back his chair and said, "Well, guys, I hate to eat
and run, but it's time I hit the sack," Binky felt herself
brighten; only then did she acknowledge how bored she'd
been feeling.

"Alan, if you eat, you *can't* run," someone said, and
Binky joined dutifully in the general laughter. But sure
enough, the party began breaking up soon after that. Binky
offered to help Doro with the dishes, but Doro said Brett
would be staying for a while to help. (From the look Brett
gave Doro, Binky deduced that this wasn't just a practical
arrangement, and wondered what time Brett would be getting home to bed. The quarterback, after all . . . Good
grief, Binky thought, am I becoming a football fan?)

Most of the others left by the kitchen door, but Piers and Binky walked back the length of the house. "I think we should thank Doro's parents, don't you?" she said. "I mean, I guess they didn't have much to do with the party, but still . . ."

"Right," Piers said, in that polite tone that was beginning to get on Binky's nerves. They passed the music room. She glanced in at the harp glimmering in the semidarkness and said, "Do you think maybe it just came with the house?" and was rewarded by a smile from Piers that made her heart give a sudden knock inside her chest. It's only because he's so ridiculously good-looking, she told herself crossly, even while she found herself smiling back at him.

They came to what Binky couldn't help thinking of as the drawing room. A few soft lights still burned, but the beautiful room was empty; the Spragues must have retired for the night, even though it was barely ten o'clock. Binky took a few steps into the room and looked around in awe. Then she said, "Piers—look!"

Above the marble fireplace was what had to be a recent portrait of Doro, but a Doro Binky was sure no one except the artist had ever seen. She wasn't quite wearing the chiffon and pearls of Binky's imagining, but the flowery green-print dress that matched her eyes was almost as romantic. There were even daisies woven through her wheat-colored hair in a kind of coronet effect.

Binky began to giggle. "Look at that smile," she said. It was more of a simper than a smile, and certainly didn't resemble any expression Binky had ever seen on Doro's no-nonsense face. "Do you suppose that's how her parents see her?" she asked Piers, more soberly.

He shrugged. "Maybe it's just how they'd like to see her. Or—who knows? maybe there's a side to Doro we don't know about."

Binky looked up at him in surprise. His face was thoughtful in a way she hadn't seen before. She considered what he'd said, and then shook her head in disagreement. "No. I think it's just to go with the house. Like the harp. I mean, you couldn't exactly hang a picture of a Cameron cheerleader over a fireplace like that. Aside from anything else, the colors wouldn't go with the room."

"No," Piers agreed, smiling a little. "I guess not."

They let themselves out the wide front door, which was latched but not bolted. "I suppose someone'll lock up later," Binky said, and added in a whisper, "Wouldn't you think they'd have a footman or two while they're at it? Or a butler, at the very least." But suddenly the big house seemed more sad than funny.

Piers seemed to feel it, too. "Weird," he said, shaking his head, and they dropped the subject.

On the ride home they made conversation for a while about the party. Piers said what a nice guy Tuck was, but didn't bring up the subject of skiing again. Binky said she thought she liked Abby the best of all the cheerleaders, except maybe for Caroline, and wasn't it too bad Caroline was dating a pompous creep like Roger. (She didn't repeat her conversation with Roger, though; the thought of it still made her burn.) She noticed that although the night air was cold and Piers had turned on the Lincoln's heater, he again slid down his window an inch or two. There was no more garlic smell; did she have bad breath, or something?

With several blocks still to go, they reverted to their other subject, football, and the prospects for tomorrow's game. (Piers didn't think they were too good.) Well, I asked for it, Binky thought, and suppressed a sigh.

But as they drew up before Binky's house, Piers' voice trailed away, as if he'd lost track of what he was saying. He turned off the ignition and said, "Did Sue speak to you about tomorrow night?" When Binky looked at him blankly, he cleared his throat and said in a kind of rush, "Well, a bunch of them are going to the rock concert over in Livingston, and they thought we might like to come along."

There were several things Binky might have said to this. "Oh, they did, did they?" and "But I hate loud rock music!" And, more important, "What about you—what do *you* think?" Because surely Piers couldn't imagine that tonight's date had been a roaring success? Or could he? Binky looked at his profile—that unreadable expression again—and realized she had no idea what Piers was thinking. Was he steeling himself against her saying no? Or against her saying yes?

Then, still looking straight ahead, Piers reached awkwardly for her hand and held it. Just a few seconds, but Binky was surprised, alarmed, and almost resentful to find that lots of little hissing rockets seemed to be shooting off colored sparks inside her head.

Was he going to kiss her now?

Before he could, and because she didn't know how she'd deal with that or even how she felt about the prospect, she found herself reaching for the door handle (or button or lever—how did the dumb thing open?) and saying, "Sure. That would be fun. Thank you for asking me, Piers."

He nodded; then, seeing her predicament, smiled a little and pressed something that released the door catch. By the time she'd extricated herself from the velvet upholstery, he had come around to escort her politely up the walk. At the door, Binky smiled up at him a little uncertainly and said, "Well, see you tomorrow," and Piers said, "Right," and turned away; and that, thought Binky, appeared to be that.

6

The painting of the Indian pipes needed something, Binky decided, studying it critically. Maybe a suggestion of moss or ferns in the background? . . . She mixed a tiny pool of gray-green, dipped her brush into it, and then laid the brush down on the tray again with a sigh. In the mood she was in, she'd probably wind up ruining the whole picture. That was the thing about watercolors—you had only one chance to get something right. You had to paint with a swift, sure hand, knowing exactly what you wanted. And this Saturday morning she felt all churned up inside.

Twice already she'd been on the point of picking up the phone to tell Piers she thought she was coming down with a cold (which was true) and would be better off staying at home after she'd done her cheerleader's stint that afternoon. The day was cold and windy, with clouds chasing each other across the sun, and she could imagine what her sinuses would feel like by the end of the afternoon—to say nothing of her throat after all the yelling she'd have to do.

An evening of pounding rock music on top of all that would probably finish her off for good.

Besides, was there really any point in seeing Piers again, when they obviously had nothing in common except, admit it, a certain physical attraction? And when it was only this whole cheerleading-football thing that had brought them together in the first place? A kind of peer pressure, in fact, Binky thought with distaste, remembering her conversation with Roger; and since when had she allowed other people to run her life?

Right. And so why hadn't she called Piers?

Binky shook her head. Restlessly, she went over to the window and looked out at the woods behind the house, where the wind was stripping the last bright leaves from the tossing treetops. It was too late now for the hog-peanut vine, but she might still be able to find a fringed gentian in bloom. . . .

She sneezed, and was forced to admit that a nice chilly tramp in the woods was the last thing she needed. Her father, at least, would be enjoying the windy weather as he flung himself off whatever cliff his hang-gliding club had chosen for today's exploits. Binky shuddered, not so much at the thought that he might hurt himself—"He has nine lives," she'd told her mother, who'd snorted and said, "Yes, and he's already used up at least eleven of them"—as at her mental image of the height, the plunge. . . . He'd taken Binky with him once last year, in one of his periodic therapy attempts. "If you have something to *do,* maybe the height won't bother you. And hang-gliding's pretty scary at first for most people. It might work out that you can transfer your fear, if you know what I mean."

But Binky hadn't been scared of hang-gliding; in fact she'd thought it looked like fun, at least when she was watching it from below. But when they climbed to the top of the cliff, one look at the new perspective was enough. She spent the rest of the time huddled against a tree trunk well back from the edge, and when it was time to leave, her father had to lead her by the hand back down the trail; no, worse than that, he had to *talk* her down, as if she were a little kid afraid of the dark. . . .

Binky backed away from the window. When she got thinking about it this way, even a two-story height could make her feel slightly giddy. She heard Dennis clomping up the stairs, and called to him, glad of a distraction. "Dennis, are you going to the library this afternoon? Because if you are, I've got a couple of books that are overdue. I'll give you the money."

"Okay." Dennis came into the room while Binky rummaged around for the books. "Too bad about your Saturday afternoons," he remarked pointedly. "One thing about basketball season, at least the games'll be at night. . . . How was the cheerleaders' party?"

Binky knew he was baiting her, but she couldn't bring herself to say she'd had a fabulous time. "It was okay," she said, and added quickly, "But you should see Doro's house —it's practically a mansion."

"Who's Doro?" Dennis was studying Binky's watercolors.

"Oh, come on, Dennis. Doro Sprague—you know, the head cheerleader. The tall blonde who's going with Brett Pastore." If Dennis asked who Brett was, Binky was ready to throw something at him.

But Dennis only grunted, leafing slowly through the paintings. "These are really good," he said. "I don't see why you aren't taking art at school. Or entering contests or something."

Binky stared at him. Dennis wanting her to enter a contest? To do something *public?* Besides, it was accepted in the family that Binky's painting was a private thing, at least for now, and not for display, least of all before teachers. But maybe Dennis didn't understand about that part of it. She said, "The last art class I took, we started with collages and ended with acrylics. The bigger and brighter and messier your stuff was, the better the teacher liked it. That meant you were being creative."

"So?"

"So what I do isn't. It's old-fashioned and boring and finicky. In fact, it's supposed to be repressed to paint the way I do. Mr. Gallagher was always telling me to express myself, and I kept telling him I *was.*" Binky sighed. "The only decent art I've gotten to do in school so far was in botany, freshman year. At least there they wanted you to draw things the way they *are,* which is what I like."

Dennis nodded. Unexpectedly, he said, "Guy I know, Mark Stevenson, I guess he's quite talented in art—well, he's taking this drawing class down at the Y, and I saw some of his stuff. It's sort of like what you do, except it's not flowers, it's oranges and vegetables and wooden bowls, like that."

"Still lifes." Binky shrugged.

"Whatever. But later I guess they'll do people—you know, have models in. Undressed, even." Dennis attempted a leer, but his fair skin could never hide a blush. "Anyway, Mark says the teacher is really good."

"I'm not interested in figure drawing," Binky said. But despite herself, she was intrigued. If it was an advanced course, as it sounded, and not just for beginners . . . She knew she needed help with perspective and with shading techniques. And she'd been wanting to learn more about charcoal, also pen-and-ink—

"When is it?" she asked. "The class, I mean."

"Saturdays, I think."

"Oh, thanks a *lot,*" Binky said, glaring at him. "Is that what all this was about—just another way of telling me I'm ruining my life by being a cheerleader? You know what, Dennis? I'm beginning to find your whole attitude extremely boring. In fact—"

"I didn't even think about the Saturday part of it until just now," Dennis interrupted hotly. "Maybe the class is first thing in the morning, *I* don't know. I was just trying to help. But if you're going to be so paranoid every time I open my mouth—"

"Paranoid! You're the one that's paranoid, acting like everything I do is some kind of threat to you, when all I'm trying to do is live my own life!"

"Oh, well, pardon me. Sure, by all means, go right ahead. Go turn cartwheels and stand on your head, the crowd'll love it. Maybe there'll even be another dog out there today for you to rescue. Or how about a stray horse? Or a lion escaped from the zoo? Go out with your jock boyfriend and let everyone talk about what a *super* couple you are. I give up. From now on I just don't care!"

He stalked out, slamming the door so hard that some of the green paint Binky had mixed earlier sloshed out of its little cup onto the bottom right-hand corner of her Indian pipe picture. There was no time to give vent to her feelings —anger, frustration, remorse—because the color was already sinking into the soft paper. Binky grabbed a brush and concentrated on transforming the stain into a semblance of a patch of moss. After a moment she mixed some yellowy brown, added a couple of toadstools, and then, in a darker copper-brown, some matted oak leaves.

She sat back and regarded the painting in pleased surprise. Much better, she saw, to use the foreground rather than the background to suggest habitat; this way it worked as a kind of botanical signature and didn't detract from the ghostly shepherd's-crook shapes of the Indian pipes themselves. Maybe she could do the same thing with her Queen-Anne's-lace picture. Yes—something simple and light-colored, a clump of bleached summer grass with a thread of purple vetch winding through it. . . .

If Liz hadn't called upstairs two hours later to say that it was after twelve and shouldn't Binky have some lunch before the game, she would have gone on painting absorbedly into the afternoon. As it was, Binky found herself standing vacantly before her closet, wondering what it was she was looking for; only when a splash of brilliant Cameron red penetrated her watercolored haze did she remember she had a different kind of afternoon's work to do. And barely time to get ready for it, she saw in alarm, yanking the skirt from its hanger and fumbling in a dresser drawer for the matching headband. Her saddle shoes were still scuffed and grass-stained from last week's game, but she couldn't take the time to whiten them. Just hope Miss Walker wouldn't notice; though she probably would.

As Binky left the room, she saw her three overdue library books—two Virginia Woolfs and a biography of Audubon—still sitting on the chair by the door. Oh, well, she thought. Some other Saturday.

Over a hasty lunch, Binky resolved to pay as little attention as possible to Piers Anderssen during today's game. She was committed to going out with him tonight, okay—but that would be the end of it. Meanwhile, the less she thought about him, or rather looked at him, the better.

But this didn't turn out to be so easy. For one thing, she couldn't help remembering what Piers had said about the rough-playing safety who was his opposite number; and all through the first quarter she found herself watching apprehensively for the foul Piers had said he would try to invite.

But this never happened, for the simple reason that before long Piers was outmaneuvering and outrunning the other boy with ease. By halftime he'd caught two touchdown passes, and with Ted Fiske kicking a successful field goal, Cameron led 17–0. And by that time everybody was watching Piers, not excluding Binky.

"Isn't he sensational?" Heather Miles enthused, as the teams left the field. "Of course, they probably didn't expect us to pass so much, what with the wind and all, but now that Brett's wrist is solid again . . . I mean, he's really throwing bullets out there. I don't see how Piers keeps catching them, except he's so fast. Do you know he never even played football until last year? Well, of course, you probably do," she said to Binky, who opened her mouth and closed it again as Heather explained to the others, "He went to some rinky-dink high school out in the Midwest somewhere, and the quarterback got hurt and they didn't have anyone else, so Piers got elected. The team wound up with a pretty good record, too."

Doro said, "Brett says that's one reason Piers is such a good receiver—because of his having played quarterback. Like when there's a foul-up on a play or Brett is getting a lot of pressure, Piers just sort of knows what his options are —Brett's, I mean." She grinned. "In fact, the way Brett was laughing and shaking his head after that last touchdown, I don't think there was anything planned about that pass. Piers just saw Brett was in trouble, and moved to where Brett had a chance of getting the ball to him."

Binky sat down on the bench, hugging herself to stop her shivers—she felt chilled through—and thought irritably that practically everything she knew about Piers Anderssen she seemed to have learned at secondhand. She looked at Heather and thought, Now there's the kind of girl Piers ought to be dating—a wholesome, uncomplicated type who's just crazy about football. (Crazy about Piers, too? Binky had her suspicions there.) Heather was the prettiest of the cheerleaders, in Binky's opinion—a tall, healthy-looking girl with thick honey-colored hair and gold-flecked gray eyes and a lovely fresh complexion. She also had stunning long legs.

Binky looked away from those legs, telling herself she wasn't envious, let alone jealous (what was there to be jealous about, for heaven's sake?), that her bad mood was only because of her stupid cold. Also, the halftime scene today had none of last week's appeal: the sky had clouded over completely, the swirling wind was tossing litter about the goalposts, and the visitors' stands across the way were only half full. The Cameron band, now performing on the field, sounded feebler and more disorganized than ever—though maybe that was partly the wind, snatching away the notes almost as soon as they were blown.

"Girls!" Binky looked up to see Mrs. Bumbry, their assistant coach, hovering in front of them with a look of concern on her plump face. The Bumble was always being concerned about something or other, to be sure; but this time it looked more urgent than usual.

"Up in the stands . . . well, I'm sure I don't have to tell you which element . . . but I'm afraid there seems to be some drinking going on. At least, two of the boys have flasks, and although they claim it's just cider, that's not what *I* smelled on their breath. I did speak to them," she added, unnecessarily, "but I'm afraid they . . . and Miss Walker's gone to speak to Frank . . . but of course we don't want any trouble. It would be much better if they just left quietly."

Binky turned to look up at the top right-hand rows of the Cameron grandstand. The "element" had dressed alike as usual in leather jackets, black jeans, and boots. In their dark

clothes, silhouetted against the murky sky, they looked like
so many crows on a fence rail, Binky thought. One of them,
a girl wearing a Black Watch plaid cap pulled down over a
tumble of dyed pinkish-red hair, was laughing uproariously
at something, but the others were sitting quietly enough.

"Cindy Brandt," Doro said with distaste, eyeing the redhead. "I hear she's practically an alcoholic these days."

"Goodness," Mrs. Bumbry said nervously. "Well, we
don't want to spread gossip, do we, dear, and anyway . . .
Oh, where has Frank got to?"

"Frank won't do anything," Sue told her. Frank was one
of the school custodians, an amiable older man who
doubled as an unofficial traffic cop on game days. "If you
really want to get rid of them, you'd better find Officer Kap-
pel. I saw him a while ago, over by the gym."

Mrs. Bumbry looked even more worried. "Oh, but police
. . . I don't think Miss Walker—or Coach Myerson—to
say nothing of Mr. Hathaway . . ." Mr. Hathaway was the
principal. Binky, who along with the others had become
adept at filling in the gaps in the Bumble's speech, understood this to mean that publicity was to be avoided at all
costs—nothing that would turn up under headlines in the
local paper.

Caroline said practically, "It must be really cold up there.
I bet they'll leave on their own if no one pressures them.
They don't exactly look like they're having a great time."

Which was true enough, Binky decided, looking back up
at the stands. She recognized Bobby Gerard, sitting mo-
rosely at the end of the row next to a girl with long, lank
blond hair and a pinched white face who looked half-frozen,
as if maybe somebody *ought* to offer her a warming gulp of
something. There was something familiar about her, Binky
thought—not that she could see the girl's features distinctly
from here, but the hair . . . that pale, solid color . . .

Could that be Piers' sister, Karen? She hoped not, but had an uneasy feeling it was.

Evidently Miss Walker had come to the same conclusion as Caroline, because when she rejoined them she said nothing about drinking going on in the stands, only told them that with Cameron so far ahead, they'd have to watch for signs of restlessness in the crowd and keep things moving. She said this with a special glance at Binky, who nodded, and wished her limbs didn't feel so leaden. But maybe she'd feel better when she got moving around again—warmer, anyhow.

Wallace Tech scored early in the third quarter, and for a while it looked as though they might catch up. But then Cameron recovered a fumble and drove into the end zone on a series of short running plays. 24–7. Binky looked up at the stands. Sure enough, no more crows. Then she saw that the blond girl had stayed behind. She'd moved down several rows and was sitting with her chin in her hands, staring out at the field. Karen, waiting for Piers to catch another touchdown pass?

If so, she was more than rewarded. A few minutes later Brett threw one of his bullets into a mass of players in the end zone, who all went down in a heap; when they disentangled themselves, it was Piers who had the ball. Binky thought he was limping a little as he came off the field. In spite of herself, she tried to catch his eye as she went through her obligatory touchdown jumps and somersaults, but as usual Piers had his eyes on the ground. If he'd looked her way at all during the game, Binky had missed it. She wasn't sure whether this was Piers being shy, wanting to avoid teasing about his supposed girlfriend, or whether it was simply the concentration of the good athlete. Most likely a combination of both, she decided; not that she cared.

Anyway, she must have been wrong about the limp, because at the beginning of the fourth quarter, Piers made the most spectacular play of the game, taking a short pass at the Wallace forty-yard line and then running all the way for a touchdown.

Except that running didn't really describe it, Binky thought. It was more like a fierce, free dance, almost like something you could set to music, as Piers eluded one tackler after another in a series of short zigs and zags, streaked along the sidelines for fifteen yards or so, spotted the Wallace safety pursuing him in a last frustrated burst of speed, spun lightly back toward the center of the field, and then floated (or so it seemed to Binky) into the end zone with the ball held high—not showing off, just demonstrating that the job was done.

And now at last the coach took him out of the game.

"Piers! Piers!" the Cameron fans chanted. Across the way, many of the Wallace Tech fans were on their feet, too, applauding. Piers was being pounded on the back by his teammates, slapped on the rump, hugged. Someone draped a warmup jacket over his shoulders. Binky watched as he edged his way over to the bench, nodding and shaking hands, and then sat down, pulling up the hood of the jacket and hunching his shoulders as if hoping he could suddenly become anonymous.

But the crowd wouldn't give up. *"Piers!"* they yelled, clapping rhythmically. *"Piers!"* At last Coach Myerson said something to Piers, and he half rose, acknowledged the cheers with a self-conscious smile and an awkward wave of his hand, and sat down again. Pandemonium. Piers hunched back into himself. Gradually the noise died away.

"Oh, Binky," Sue said. "Aren't you *proud?*"

Proud? What did it have to do with her? Even if she'd been Piers' lifelong girlfriend, Binky couldn't imagine taking any part of the credit for an achievement that belonged to Piers alone. Was she supposed to have *inspired* him or something? Or was this just what people meant when they talked about reflected glory? Because if so—

But before she could set Sue straight, Doro was beckoning the cheerleaders over to her. "Okay, guys," she said. "Now we really go to work."

"We do?" Binky looked at the scoreboard, which read CAMERON 31, VISITORS 7. It seemed to her they might as well all go home.

"The big routines," Doro explained. "The fancy stuff we've been working on. Now's the time to bring it on, before people get bored. We'll start with the Swallow Dive."

The Swallow Dive was a pyramid stunt which called for the person on top, Binky in this case, to perform an interrupted double flip. The moment she took off into the first one, Caroline and Lynette beneath her peeled away into side cartwheels, while Abby, in the bottom row, rose from a half-kneeling position, took two steps forward, and set her shoulders so that Binky could spring from them into her second flip—landing lightly in front of them all with her arms raised in a V salute. The trick was in the successive releases: Caroline and Lynette had to move quickly in order to free Abby and give her time to get in position.

Everyone looked a little apprehensive, but Doro said firmly, "It'll go fine. Binky, just remember to count five, loud and clear, before you take off, to make sure everyone's set—okay?"

Okay.

Binky lost all track of time after that—of time and gravity and even the weather. If it had started snowing, she probably wouldn't even have noticed. Her throat hurt, and her head felt oddly light, precariously attached to the rest of her. On the other hand, her saddle shoes seemed to weigh thirty pounds apiece. Thank God for what she thought of as the "body memory" she'd developed in gymnastics. If she'd had to depend on her brain alone for the complex sequence of movements she was called on to perform, with their split-second rhythm and timing, she'd probably have wound up crippling herself or one of her teammates.

When the clock ran out at last, Binky lay down flat on the cold grass, feeling she never wanted to move again.

"You okay?" Lynette said, peering down at her.

"Just a cold," Binky croaked. "I swear, we've worked harder than the players today."

"Well, sure. I'm always telling Richard I'm in better shape than he is. You better get to the showers, Binky. I mean, you want to be okay for tonight."

"Tonight," Binky repeated numbly.

"You and Piers—you're coming to the concert, aren't you? After all, the Man of the Hour . . ." Lynette smirked at her.

Binky groaned. Right. The Man of the Hour—you couldn't let him down, could you? No, you couldn't. Not at the last minute, not even if you were developing walking pneumonia. She took the hand Lynette extended to her and pulled herself painfully to her feet.

Piers looked at their tickets as they edged their way into the jammed lobby of the sports arena where the rock concert was being held. "I guess we're up in the balcony," he told Binky.

"Oh, lucky you," Sue said. They'd given Sue and Alan a ride over to Livingston—not in a Lincoln this time but in a Volvo wagon Piers said belonged to his mother. "We're way down front. The balcony's a lot more fun."

Binky wondered if it was a very high balcony, then decided she felt too rotten to care. Maybe that's my cure, she thought; next time Dad wants to get me up on top of a mountain, I'll wait until I'm in the advanced stages of bubonic plague or typhoid fever. . . . Her mother had dosed her with hot lemon and honey, and Binky had finally given in and taken an antihistamine to stop herself sneezing, much as she hated taking pills; also so her eyes wouldn't look quite so red and watery. Glamor might be beyond her, but the least she could do was try to make Piers a presentable date. To that end she had also changed her clothes three times, and was already regretting the choice of an angora sweater. The soft rose color was becoming, but the little drifting hairs kept tickling her nose.

Piers looked from Binky to Sue. "Do you want to trade seats?" he asked. "I don't mind sitting downstairs, if Binky doesn't."

Binky shook her head confusedly. Had her face given something away? But at the moment she really didn't care where they sat. Sue accepted the trade eagerly, and she and Alan pushed their way toward the long ramp that led to the top of the arena.

Only as she and Piers headed down the aisle toward their seats did Binky have an inkling of why Piers had wanted to make the switch: he was limping. Or rather, he was trying not to limp. She could feel it because he was holding her elbow to help steer her through the crowd of kids; she doubted anyone could see it. And in fact, they were attracting a good deal of attention by the time they reached the front rows. This was partly because of the striking couple they made, Binky was resignedly aware, remembering the newspaper photo; but also because there were a lot of Cameron students in the audience.

"Look, there's Piers . . . you know, Piers Anderssen, the one who . . . And Binky Nolan, yeah, the cute little cheerleader, the one who . . . Hey, Piers, great game! Hi, Binky! . . . Hey, Anderssen, way to go!"

Binky had expected something like this, but hadn't thought it would feel so much like a royal progress. Heads were turning, and someone was actually applauding. She nodded and smiled as casually as she could, while Piers looked straight ahead. The tips of his ears were pink, she noticed, just like Dennis' when he was embarrassed.

Their seats were in the third row, way over on the left—in fact the last two seats in the row, Binky discovered gratefully, squeezing past pairs of knees. If she began feeling peculiar again, she could lean against the wall. She saw Piers grimace as he sat down beside her, shifting his weight as if trying to find a comfortable position.

"Piers, what's the matter with your leg?" she asked in a low voice. "You hurt it this afternoon, didn't you?" When he just shrugged, she said accusingly, "You shouldn't have come tonight."

Piers smiled faintly. "Neither should you, with your cold."

"Oh, a cold—" But Binky spoiled the effect by sneezing suddenly. So much for the antihistamine, she thought in vexation.

"It's just a hamstring," Piers said. "Nothing much."

"Just a hamstring!" said Binky, who knew otherwise. "You should be home keeping ice on it. Why didn't you call me?"

But as soon as she asked the question, she thought she knew the answer: Piers hadn't wanted to spoil her evening any more than she'd wanted to spoil his. Or was it that? Piers seemed to consider the subject closed; he was gazing at the stage, where the musicians were testing mikes and instruments, kicking aside snaky coils of wire with the toes of their high-heeled boots. Maybe Piers was just crazy about rock music.

For something to say, and without considering how she was going to pursue it, Binky said, "I think I saw your sister at the game today. Karen—isn't that her name? Thin, with long blond hair? She was with—" Binky stopped abruptly.

"I know who she was with." Piers' voice was toneless.

"Well, anyway," Binky said—babbling again, as she always seemed to when he got that wooden look on his face— "I guess she must be really proud of you. That one super run you made, especially—"

"My sister hates football," Piers interrupted, still staring straight ahead. "Or anyway, she hates my playing football. She only goes to the games because of those creeps she hangs out with, and they're not exactly your ordinary fans."

Binky was taken aback. More than that, she was sure Piers was wrong, remembering how Karen had stayed on alone; remembering the intent, somehow forlorn way she had sat gazing down at the field.

"But Piers," she began—and was drowned out by an ear-splitting wail of amplified sound. The concert had begun.

After a while Binky wondered why she'd bothered to worry about sneezing or coughing throughout the concert, since no one could possibly have heard her. As for red eyes —who would notice them, the way the pulsing lights kept turning faces blue, purple, green, and orange in lurid succession? The lights, more than the music, made Binky's head begin to ache. She wished she had a pair of dark glasses. She closed her eyes, but opened them again when Piers jostled her shoulder, muttering an apology. The two seats on his other side had been vacant, but now a pair of latecomers were squeezing into them. Binky was crammed further against the wall, which at least gave her a good excuse for resting her heavy head against it.

The band wasn't really too bad, she decided drowsily. From a distance of, say, half a mile, they might have sounded quite good. . . . Now her eyelids were closing of their own volition. She made herself open them again, and noticed how rigidly Piers was sitting, and also—as a band of orange light illuminated his features—that he was sweating lightly. The exit doors, which had stood partly open, guarded by cops, while the arena was filling, were closed now; but the building had good ventilation, or so it seemed to Binky. In fact, she felt a bit chilly, but maybe that was because of her cold. Piers wasn't even wearing a sweater, just a lightweight flannel shirt; his Cameron jacket hung over the back of his seat.

He must be in a lot more pain than he'd let on, Binky thought. She felt remorseful for a moment—but really, why should she? It was his own fault for being so stubborn. Anyway, there's nothing I can do about it now, Binky thought. The way we're all crammed into this place, you'd need a battering ram to get out of it. At intermission, maybe. . . . Binky drew her own jacket up around her shoulders and settled herself more comfortably against the wall, wishing it wouldn't thud so with each reverberation of the drums. Or maybe that was the people up in the balcony stamping their feet. She was glad after all not to be sitting in the balcony. . . .

At intermission Piers woke her up.

"Oh, my gosh," Binky said, blinking at him. But he was grinning.

"Let's get out of here," he said. "You ought to be home in bed."

Binky wondered if she'd been snoring, and if so, whether he'd noticed. Her tongue felt thick, and she yawned before she could stop herself. Making an effort, she said, "But what about Sue and Alan?"

"They can go home with Lynette and Richard," Piers said firmly, helping her up. He winced as he straightened his leg.

"The walking wounded," Binky said drowsily, and yawned again. "Ouch, my throat hurts."

"So don't talk," Piers told her, edging them along toward the aisle. "I suppose you had that cold all day, and you still went out and yelled your head off at the game."

"Well, *you* were hurt after that second touchdown—or was it the third—and you still stayed in the game," Binky said. "Yes, you were, I saw you limping. And then you made that wonderful run . . . did I tell you how beautiful that was, Piers?" Binky knew she was babbling again, but this time it was because she felt so light-headed. Maybe she was allergic to antihistamine? "It was one of the most fabulous things I ever saw. Just . . . fabulous."

Piers gave her a quick smile—a real smile, as she thought of it hazily, that narrowed the corners of his blue eyes and showed his crooked front tooth. He put an arm around her shoulders, steadying her. "Onward," he said, and piloted her the short distance to the exit door.

The cold night air revived Binky for the few minutes it took them to walk to the car. She found herself making inane conversation about the band—the girl vocalist was really quite good, wasn't she, and the second guitarist, too, the one with the green moustache, not the one with the ponytail—to which Piers replied with the grunts these remarks deserved.

But once in the car, she fell asleep again, and woke only when they drew up in front of her house. At least, Binky thought in embarrassment, she hadn't conked out with her head on Piers' shoulder—if only because of her seat belt (she didn't remember fastening it; Piers must have done that). Now she fumbled for the clasp with heavy fingers, shook her head to clear it, and said, "Some date I turned out to be. I'm really sorry, Piers. . . . How does your leg feel?"

"Lousy," Piers said, turning toward her. He cupped her face in his hands and kissed her gently on the lips.

"You'll get my cold," Binky protested, feeling several kinds of alarm at once.

"I don't care," he said, and kissed her again.

"Piers . . ." Binky drew back, looking up into his grave face. "Enough," she said, as lightly as she could. "I think sleep really *is* what I need, so . . . so just stop waking me up, will you?"

For a moment she thought she'd offended him. Then his expression softened. He smiled and said, "Okay. I'll call you tomorrow." He opened the door, levered himself cautiously out of the car, and limped around to Binky's side to escort her decorously, once again, to her front door.

7

Binky slept until noon the next day and woke up feeling much better, only to find the rest of her family in a foul mood, for assorted reasons. Her mother was mad at her father because he'd come home from hang-gliding with a broken big toe. The fact that this had occurred when the club van had a flat tire on the way home and the jack fell over onto his foot—"an accident that could happen to anybody"—didn't mollify her. Her father was mad because the toe hurt a lot and also because he had an important presentation to make at the office next day. "I have enough trouble with all the ridiculous jargon I'm expected to produce without having to appear in *slippers*," he said. "I'll start laughing. Or maybe crying. Either way, it'll be a disaster."

"Cry," Liz said nastily. "It'll go over better."

Dennis was mad because . . . well, Binky wasn't quite sure why, except that a phone call from a friend seemed to have something to do with it. He looked so thunderous that finally she swallowed her pride and apologized for having flared up at him the day before. "I guess I was overreacting," she said. "I'd really like to find out about that art class, Dennis, if you'll ask your friend for me." He nodded, but remained tight-lipped. Binky gave up and went back to her painting.

Only when Sue called to find out how she was feeling did Binky begin to have an idea of what was bothering Dennis.

"That was quite an exit you made last night," Sue said, giggling. "You and Piers, I mean. Of course, *I* knew you weren't feeling too good, and that was probably why he had his arm around you and everything. But it sure looked like . . . well, you know."

"No," Binky said grimly. "I don't know. What *did* it look like?"

"Oh, come on, Binky—leaving in the middle of the concert in that lovey-dovey way, heading for the nearest exit without even speaking to anyone. . . . I mean, everybody figured you two just couldn't wait to be alone together."

"Everybody," Binky repeated, her heart sinking.

Sue said, "Binky, don't you realize that you and Piers are, well, sort of celebrities? Each of you on your own, I mean; and then, when you're together—it's the super-couple thing, like the paper said. What I mean is, people *notice* you. But never mind, it's what's between you and Piers that really counts. . . . Have you heard from him today?" she asked, lowering her voice intimately.

"No," Binky said. "Listen, Sue, I have to go."

"Oh, sure. I'll get off the line, he might be trying to call you. See you tomorrow—glad you're feeling better. Gosh . . ." Sue giggled again. "I hope Piers doesn't get your cold. I mean, that would really sort of—"

"Good-bye, Sue," Binky said firmly, and hung up.

With friends like Sue Streibeck, she thought, marching back to her room, who needs enemies? She grabbed her sketch pad and a pencil and drew a furious caricature of Sue, something she often did when she was mad at someone —snub nose, round eyes, brainless smile—then crumpled up the page and threw both it and the pencil into the wastebasket. After a moment she retrieved the pencil, which was a good soft-leaded one. With most of her savings gone and no time for baby-sitting because of cheerleading, she couldn't afford to throw away expensive art supplies.

Binky sat down on her bed with her head in her hands. She supposed she should be grateful to Sue for warning her, if "everybody" really was saying . . . But how dare they? And what business was it of theirs, anyway? Did Piers know? And if so—

The phone rang again. This time Dennis answered it.

"It's for you," he said. "Piers."

He handed her the receiver as if it were contaminated. Binky clapped her hand over the mouthpiece and hissed, "Dennis, I don't care what people are saying, we only left the concert early because of my cold. I fell asleep during it!" She could see he didn't believe her. How could anybody fall asleep in the middle of a rock concert? "I came straight home—you must have heard me come in."

"I went to bed early," Dennis said stonily. "Anyway, it's none of my business." He stalked away.

Binky took a deep breath and raised the phone to her ear. "Hello, Piers."

"Hello. How's your cold?"

"Better. How's your leg?"

"Better."

Oh, great, Binky thought. Another one of our brilliant conversations. She struggled for a fresh topic. The weather? Football? But next week's game was too far away to be a very immediate subject. Of course there was yesterday's game. . . . "I guess your name is all over the sports page today," she said brightly, though she hadn't even looked at the paper.

"I guess."

Wrong thing to say, Binky realized. One of the few things she knew about Piers was that he honestly disliked publicity, maybe even more so than she did herself.

He cleared his throat. "Ah . . . there's a dance at school on Saturday. I don't know what time we'll get back from Glenville"—next week's was an away game—"but if it's not too late . . . well, would you like to go?"

Binky told herself that the sensible thing would be to refuse politely. But there were several problems with that. First, she couldn't think of a good excuse on the spur of the moment. Second, she was afraid she might be saying no just to prove that "everybody" was wrong about her and Piers; and no way was Binky Nolan going to start letting other people's opinions dictate what she did or didn't do. Third, this was the first time Piers had asked her out on his own, a date involving just the two of them, nothing to do with football players and cheerleaders. . . . Binky wondered if Piers was a good dancer, and decided he probably wasn't.

"Okay," she heard herself saying, instead of "Well, I'm not sure" or "Can I let you know?" as she'd half intended to. "That would be fun."

"Right. Well . . . take care of yourself."

"You, too."

End of conversation. Binky looked around for Dennis, hoping perversely that he'd been listening in; a less romantic or (she shuddered) lovey-dovey exchange could hardly be imagined. But he was nowhere to be seen.

Within a few weeks Piers and Binky were an established couple, not only in the eyes of their public but in their own as well. Just how this had come about, Binky wasn't quite sure. In trying to assert her independence, she also, confusingly, seemed to have wound up following the path of least resistance. She said as much to Spencer, in one of their infrequent conversations; they were friends again, in a wary sort of way. He grinned—it was just the sort of paradox Spencer enjoyed—and said, "Might as well relax and just go with it, Bink. I mean, never mind outside pressures, you've got to admit there's a certain irresistible logic about the whole thing. The football star and the cheerleader . . . well, why not, at least for the duration of the football season?"

Was that how Piers felt? Binky didn't know. In fact, his motivation was even less clear to her than her own. Their dates were anything but exciting. Conversation continued to consist mostly of near-monosyllables on Piers' part and chatter (usually just to fill the vacuum) on Binky's. When they saw a movie, it was Binky who talked about it afterward, Piers' contribution being confined to statements like "pretty good," "not bad," and "okay, I guess." As Binky had suspected, Piers was a poor dancer, stiff and tentative, all his natural grace left behind on the football field. When they went out for pizza—and this was the kind of thing Binky found particularly maddening, for some reason—Piers always ordered the same kind: cheese, period. She couldn't get him to try even a bite of her own pepperoni or sausage. Same thing with ice cream: chocolate chip for Piers, every single time.

Yet within twenty-four hours of each mostly boring evening, Piers was on the phone setting up another one. He never asked her for the next date at the end of the evening because . . . well, because that part *wasn't* boring, and in fact after they got to kissing for a while, it was hard to remember even what day it was, let alone make plans for the future. At least that was true for Binky, and she assumed it was true for Piers, too. In fact, she thought they were both a little scared by their own sensations during these sessions, so that they never went on too long (or too far). Well, again, this was a deduction on Binky's part, based on the way they always seemed to draw apart at the same moment—the way Piers cleared his throat and said, "Well—" in a husky voice, and Binky said, "I know," and they both laughed a little, self-consciously, before Piers reached for the handle of the car door. . . .

Binky's cheeks burned whenever she thought about this aspect of their relationship, hoping it wasn't the main one—the reason she kept saying yes to each date. And the reason Piers kept asking her. Because if it was, she felt . . . well, cheap.

She tried to talk to her mother about this. Liz said she didn't really think "cheap" came into it. "Natural" was more like it. "He's a very attractive boy, after all," she said. "I'd be worried if you *didn't* like kissing him."

"But . . . but the rest of the time it's like we're not even on the same wavelength," Binky had protested.

"Well, look at your father and me," Liz said, with a shrug. "We disagree about almost everything."

"Oh, Mom"—Binky had to smile—"that's not the same thing, and you know it. You're crazy about each other. *I* know that. Dennis knows that."

Liz looked relieved. "Well, thank heavens. Sometimes, with all the sniping we do at each other, I've wondered. . . . But anyway, my point is that even if you and Piers don't see eye to eye about a lot of things—"

"But it's not like that," Binky interrupted. "I mean, we don't have *fights,* Mom. I don't know him well enough to have a fight with him—don't you see?" When her mother looked puzzled, Binky explained, "I don't even know what Piers thinks about most things. Either he doesn't want me to know, or—or he just doesn't think anything! He doesn't even have a sense of humor. Well, that's not true, exactly— he'll smile at other people's jokes, but he never makes any himself. He never tries to be *entertaining,* if you know what I mean."

Liz pondered this for a while. "Well," she admitted, "he doesn't sound exactly like scintillating company. . . . Maybe he just needs more scope. Someone to draw him out. For instance, he and your father always seem to find plenty to talk about when he comes to pick you up—"

"Oh, sure," Binky said. "About ice-boating and skiing and hockey players."

"Well, I know, but—Binky, why don't you invite Piers to dinner some night soon? Maybe in a relaxed family situation . . . You could cook one of your three-star meals, if you want," Liz said generously. "I'd stay out of your way."

"Piers doesn't like fancy food."

"Then cook him a steak," Liz said, in some exasperation. "The food isn't the point, anyway. Just put it on the basis that we'd like to get to know him better."

"Including Dennis?" Binky shook her head.

"Especially including Dennis. In fact, if Dennis could see Piers as more than a football player, more than his sister's boyfriend. . . . He's still scared of sex, you know, Binky, and he's not used to thinking of you as—well, a female person, with all that implies. When he starts taking girls out on his own, he'll look at things differently, but for now—"

"For now, he thinks I reek of it," Binky said bitterly. "Well, maybe I do."

"Binky . . ." Liz sighed, smiled, and gave her daughter a hug. "Back to square one, it seems. Listen, stop worrying, will you? I know you, and I trust you. Not only that you'll . . . keep things under control, but that if you really decide there's nothing more than physical attraction between you and Piers, you'll stop seeing him."

"If only I didn't like *looking* at him so much," Binky said unhappily, not at all sure her mother was right. But in the end she promised, reluctantly, to invite Piers over for dinner some night soon.

As it happened, though, it was Binky who was invited to the Anderssens' while she was still stalling over her own invitation; in fact, while she'd just about decided there was no point in issuing it anyway. Piers' parents were giving a big party on the Sunday of Thanksgiving weekend, and thought it would be nice, Piers said, relaying the message rather stiffly, if he invited his girl.

"You mean to help pass things, and stuff?" Binky asked, and added quickly, "Not that I mind."

What she did mind was that she'd half planned—no, *had* planned—to tell Piers tonight that she thought they should stop seeing so much of each other.

It was the evening of the Big Game against Livingston, the last of the season, which Cameron had lost by twenty points. She and Piers were on their way to a party, or non-party, at Heather's. Binky wasn't looking forward to it much, and didn't think anyone else could be, either, but it seemed to be something you had to do, win or lose, on Big Game night.

Anyway, since it *was* the end of the season, this had seemed to Binky a logical time to cool things with Piers, or . . . or at least to have a talk about their relationship. If she said yes to his parents' invitation, she'd be committing herself for another whole week in a way that didn't seem fair to Piers.

On the other hand, she thought uncertainly, maybe her timing was a bit crude. They'd lost the game, after all, and although Piers had played well, he *had* dropped a long pass in the third quarter which just might have made a crucial difference. Not that he seemed particularly downcast; in fact, Binky had a distinct impression that he, too, was relieved the football season was over. Still, he must be feeling pretty sore and tired tonight.

Also, Binky couldn't help being curious about his family, whom she'd never met.

"Oh, no," Piers said, in answer to her question about helping out at the party. "Nothing like that. It's being catered. All anyone has to do is show up." His voice was toneless, and his profile had that set look which Binky had learned by now to interpret as a sign that he was unhappy about something. She'd also learned that there was no point in asking him what it was.

"Well, that's nice of your parents," Binky said. She decided to temporize. "Can I let you know? I'm not sure what my family has planned for that Sunday. We'll be having houseguests." This was true enough—old friends who always spent Thanksgiving weekend with them. But they were hardly the kind of guests you had to stick around for. The wife was a professional violinist who always spent hours practicing up in the guest room, and the husband, an art historian, was into motorcycles (in fact, they always traveled by motorcycle, which made Binky worry about the violin); he and her father would spend most of their time zooming around on it while her mother smoldered over the Thanksgiving fixings.

Piers shrugged and said sure, no big deal. But Binky saw how his hands tightened on the steering wheel (they were in a Lincoln again, a beige one this time). Was he already sensing her withdrawal? Was it really going to bother him that much? Oh, dear, Binky thought despondently, I should never have let things go on this long. It's going to be harder than I thought.

Maybe harder on her, too, as she discovered a few minutes later when Heather greeted them at the door. "Oh, Piers, I'm so *sorry* about the game," she said. She looked it, too, Binky thought—almost in tears. She also looked particularly fetching in a bright-red peasant-style dress that suited her glowing good looks. (Cameron red? Well, not quite, but a nice try, Binky decided.)

"They had a better team," Piers said simply. Binky thought that this was the kind of thing she really admired about Piers. She also thought, noticing the way Heather's eyes lingered wistfully on Piers' face, that there was nothing she despised more than a dog-in-the-manger. . . .

But somehow she found herself going to the Anderssens' party.

Piers had to be outside at first, helping park cars, so Binky got her father to drive her over. "*Not* on the motorcycle, Dad," she said firmly, indicating her good winter-white wool dress and new beige pumps.

Binky had seen the Anderssens' house just once before, when Piers stopped by for something on one of their dates. He'd only been a minute, and she'd stayed in the car. It was a sleek, expensive-looking split-level in the newer part of town. Today, in the chill November dusk of late afternoon, it looked quite festive, lights blazing from every window. There was already a large Christmas wreath on the front door, Binky saw.

"Well, here you are," her father said. "Ready to mingle with the town's finest—everybody who's anybody, it looks like," he added, nodding toward several fur-coated ladies and their well-tailored escorts who were making their way up the flagstone walk. "I hear Hal Anderssen's doing well with that dealership. A finger in several other pies, too, so they say. . . ." He looked thoughtful for a moment; then gave Binky's shoulder a little push. "Onward, Cinderella. Any of your other friends going to be here?"

"I don't think so," Binky said uncertainly. "It's really for adults. Except I guess Piers' sister will be around. . . . Piers said just to go in, he'd come as soon as he could." Now she caught a glimpse of him in the driveway, waving directions at someone who was about to back his car into a clump of rhododendrons.

"So go," her father said. "Me, I can't wait to get back to the cold turkey, greasy fingers and all."

Binky approached the front door a little nervously; but she'd hardly taken a step into the hall, which smelled of perfume and hothouse roses, before she was greeted by a large, red-faced man with a glass in one hand who shook her hand vigorously with the other, beamed at her, and said, "Well, Binky! Pleased to meet you at long last. Course I've seen you many times on the football field, but you never stopped jumping up and down long enough for me to get a good look at you. But Piers was right, you're a real winner. I'm Hal Anderssen," he explained superfluously.

Binky smiled back in some confusion. Piers had never mentioned his father's coming to games; nor could she imagine his describing her in such terms . . . describing her at all, in fact. But before she could think of a response, Mr. Anderssen said, "Here, let Karen take your coat, and then let's get you something to drink. . . . You know Karen, of course," he added, indicating the slender, thin-faced blond girl who came forward sulkily, carrying several other coats over her arm.

"Hi," Binky said.

Karen nodded stonily, in a way that reminded Binky of Dennis, not meeting Binky's eyes.

Binky surrendered her coat, and was ushered into a big,

crowded living room with a bar at the far end. "Now, what
will you have? Coke, ginger ale—or how about a glass of
sherry? I've got some nice, dry stuff, smooth as silk, you'll
hardly feel it going down—Spanish, of course, a friend of
mine imports it especially for my cellar. And let's see, I've
got a sweeter brand, too, I know a lot of you kids prefer
sweet drinks—"

"Ginger ale would be fine, thanks," Binky said.

"Well, fine, fine," Mr. Anderssen echoed, as heartily as if
she'd turned out to be a connoisseur of his "cellar." He took
her elbow. "Now all we have to do is steer a path through
this mob. Told my wife she was overdoing the guest list, but
of course she wouldn't listen . . . she's crazy to meet you,
by the way. . . ."

But halfway to the bar he was distracted by a group of
friends, and Binky proceeded alone to get her ginger ale
from a white-coated bartender. A maid was passing hot
hors d'oeuvres, and Binky, who was hungry, helped herself
to several. They weren't as good as they looked, she thought
critically; she herself made a lighter cheese puff, and the
bacon sticks ought to have been left under the broiler a
minute longer. . . .

She stood sipping her ginger ale and looking at all the
people, trying to figure out which one was Mrs. Anderssen
so that she could introduce herself. Get it over with, was
what she found herself thinking, because really this wasn't
her kind of scene at all. She didn't recognize anyone among
this crowd of dressed-up people (her good wool dress suddenly seemed much too casual), and their cigarette smoke
was making her eyes sting. Her own parents never gave
cocktail parties and avoided going to them except when her
father's business demanded it. Their idea of a party was to
invite six or eight assorted friends and acquaintances over
for wine and cheese and maybe a hunk of good pâté if they

were feeling flush. Such parties usually ended up with everyone sitting around the kitchen table, laughing and arguing. Binky couldn't imagine this one ending that way.

"Hi. You get something to drink okay?" Piers appeared beside her, and suddenly Binky felt much better—if only, she told herself, because he looked even more glorious than usual in a sky-blue sport coat with a white shirt and a gray-patterned tie that matched his flannels. Binky had never seen Piers in a collar and tie before. There was fresh color in his cheeks from the outside air, and his hair was slightly roughened. It took her a moment to realize how tense he was.

"Your father wanted me to have sherry," she said, and saw his mouth tighten. "But I didn't think I'd like it. . . . Piers, where's your mother? I haven't met her yet."

Piers surveyed the room, which was really jammed now with new arrivals. "Over by the fireplace," he said. "Come on." He took Binky's hand. Looking in the direction he'd indicated, Binky saw a tall, rather haughty-looking blond woman in an embroidered mauve tunic outfit who seemed to be holding court among a cluster of guests. That must be where Piers gets his looks, she thought, a little apprehensively, as they squeezed their way forward. Binky Nolan, ma'am, reporting for inspection. . . .

But to her surprise Piers was turning to a small, plumpish woman in a gold brocade dress which had probably cost plenty but which did nothing for her. If her hair had once been blond, it was now gray—or rather, a kind of sallow grayish-blond, as if she'd had an unsuccessful rinse. But her eyes were the same pure blue as Piers'; she also, Binky noticed, had the same look of strain around the mouth.

"Mom, this is Binky," Piers said, his voice unexpectedly gentle.

Mrs. Anderssen produced a smile, but Binky felt she

wasn't really seeing her. The blue eyes looked slightly glazed, and the hand she held out to Binky was ice-cold—though that might have been from the glass she was holding. But her voice was soft. "It was nice of you to come, Binky," she said—and for a moment her eyes did seem to focus, her smile warmed, almost shyly. "So nice for Piers. . . ."

"Well, it was nice of you to ask me, Mrs. Anderssen," Binky said awkwardly. "It seems like a—a nice party." "Nice" again! What was wrong with her? Binky was rarely at a loss for words, but something about this woman—

Piers said, "Do you want me to try moving some people into the dining room, Mom? It's getting pretty crowded in here."

"The dining room," she said vaguely, taking a sip of her drink. "Yes, I suppose the buffet must be ready by now . . . that would be nice of you, Piers." She held out her hand to Binky, as though forgetting she'd already done so. "Well, you young people enjoy yourselves. I'm sorry there aren't more of you, but Karen—My husband didn't seem to feel her friends—"

"It's okay, Mom," Piers said quickly. "Don't worry about us. We're just fine."

Mrs. Anderssen nodded, smiled distractedly, and turned back to her other guests. Binky supposed it must be quite a responsibility, giving a big party like this, but still . . . "Piers—" she began questioningly.

"Do you want another ginger ale?" he asked abruptly. "Because if you don't—"

"No, you go ahead and do your herding, or whatever," Binky said, looking up at him in some perplexity. "I think I'll sort of edge back toward the hall. It's awfully smoky in here."

"Sure. Listen, I'm sorry, I'll get back to you as soon as I

can. Maybe—" He hesitated, then said in a rush, "Maybe you could go talk to my sister. You know, get acquainted. Like Mom said, there aren't any other young people here, so—"

"Well, sure," Binky said, but added, remembering the look of hostility on Karen's face, "only I don't know exactly what we'll talk about. Of course, there's always you, if worse comes to worst."

But Piers didn't return her smile. "Talk to her about—about writing," he said, and turned away.

Writing? Or had he said "riding"? Binky shook her head bemusedly as she set off in search of Karen. Well, considering that she knew very little about either subject, perhaps it didn't matter; considering, too, that Karen had shown no sign of wanting to talk to Binky. Maybe she was jealous of her brother's having a girlfriend, the way Dennis was of Binky's dating Piers, Binky thought uncertainly.

It was a relief, anyway, to escape into the relative coolness and quiet of the front hall, though Binky found the smell of the roses—huge pink ones massed in silver bowls—a bit overpowering. After a moment she noticed a half-open door leading into what seemed to be a study. She edged through it tentatively and found Karen sitting in a leather armchair, her shoes kicked off and her legs drawn up under her, reading a book. She glanced up as Binky entered, then immediately returned her eyes to the page.

"Hi," Binky said, wasting her biggest smile on the empty air. "Do you mind if I sit down here for a few minutes?" A barely perceptible shrug. "It's a nice party, but it's getting kind of noisy. Besides, my feet are killing me. New shoes—you know."

"It's not a nice party," Karen said into her book, ignoring this last. "It's a terrible party. My parents' parties always are."

Binky couldn't think of any reply to this, and decided to throw charm to the winds in favor of a direct approach. She sat down on a leather hassock. "Piers says you're interested in writing," she said. (On the evidence of the book this seemed more likely than riding, at any rate.)

If she'd wanted eye contact, she got it now—a stare of cold fury from eyes that were a paler blue than Piers', and, at the moment, much harder.

"So?" Karen said. "I don't see that it's any business of yours."

Binky considered this for a moment. "No," she agreed. "It was just something to talk about. What kind of writing do you do?"

Karen drew an angry breath; for a moment Binky was sure she wasn't going to answer. Then she tossed the book onto the floor, where it landed facedown, leaned back, and said coldly, "I write poetry. Bad poetry. I also get straight A's on all my school papers. My family thinks I ought to take 'creative writing' "—she put the words in scornful quotes—"to develop my so-called talent. But the way they teach it here, all it amounts to is making mud pies out of words."

Binky smiled a little, thinking of art classes. Karen noticed, and misinterpreted the smile. "I know," she said. "Futile, aren't I? But then, I don't have the talent to be anything as *creative* as a cheerleader. On the other hand . . ." She regarded Binky for a thoughtful moment, twisting a strand of hair around her finger; Binky noticed that it needed washing. "You're a friend of Spencer Bryant's, right? Sure, that must be what Piers had in mind. So okay." Her gaze was both hostile and challenging. "Get me a job on the school paper."

Binky was taken aback. "I don't think Piers . . . well, never mind that. But anyway, I can't do that, Karen. I mean, that's not the way it works. They hold tryouts in the spring, there's a regular system—"

"Oh, there's always a system," Karen interrupted. "And there are always ways to beat it. *If* you know the right people. So you tell Spencer Bryant that your boyfriend's little sister needs rehabilitating—is that the way Piers put it? —and also that she can write rings around most of the people he's got working for him. I can, too."

"I'm sure you can," Binky said uncomfortably. "But I told you, Karen, that's not the way it works. I could mention you to Spencer and tell him you're interested in the paper, but you'd still have to try out when the time comes. I'm sorry, but I really can't do much more than that."

"Can't? Or won't?" Karen's thin face wore a curious mixture of anger and satisfaction. "Oh, well," she said, pushing herself out of the armchair, "I just thought you might be good for *something*. Wrong again."

She left the room, not quite slamming the door behind her. Binky sat stunned, not so much by what Karen had said as by the bitterness behind it. And I think I have troubles with Dennis! she thought. After a moment she reached for the abandoned book and saw, with a little start, that it was a copy of Virginia Woolf's *To the Lighthouse.* If only she'd begun by asking Karen what she was reading . . . but maybe it wouldn't have made any difference. Absently, Binky picked up one of Karen's shoes and turned it over in her hands—a pretty shade of midnight blue, brand-new like her own, not a scuff mark on it.

"Well, well. I gather you girls have been having a little chat." Mr. Anderssen looked in the doorway, again with glass in hand, smiling his buoyant smile. "Glad to see that. Fine girl like you, Binky, just the sort of friend Karen needs. She's been having a few problems—new town, new school, you know how it is. But there's good stuff in Karen, she'll straighten out all right." He took a hefty swallow of his drink.

"Yes. I mean, I'm sure. . . ." For the second time that evening Binky felt at a loss for words. She also felt rather foolish, sitting there on the hassock with the book and one of Karen's blue shoes on her lap.

But before she could think of something suitably dignified to do or say, Mr. Anderssen glanced over his shoulder and said, "Ah, here's the son and heir himself. Everything going all right out there?"

"Sure, Dad." Piers came into the room carrying two plates of food from the buffet. His eyes registered Karen's absence and moved quickly to Binky, who shook her head slightly.

"Good, good. Well, back to my duties. Little Binky here, she's a sight for sore eyes, but"—he heaved a sigh—"I guess I'd better act my age and go join the rest of the old fogies." He gave Binky a wink and a broad grin. "See you kids later."

"Piers," Binky began urgently, as soon as his father had closed the door, ignoring the plate Piers held out to her, "I'm afraid I blew it with your sister. She certainly doesn't like me very much, in fact she—Well, never mind that now. The thing is, she wanted me to get her a job on the school paper, because of knowing Spencer, and I said I couldn't, not just like that, and—and, well, I'm afraid she's kind of upset. Maybe you should go talk to her."

Piers regarded the polished tips of his loafers for a long moment. Then he set Binky's plate down on a low table near her and began applying himself to his own, leaning up against the mantel. "She's always upset about something," he said, spearing a slice of ham. "I wouldn't take it personally."

Suddenly furious, Binky got to her feet, toppling the book

and shoe back onto the floor. "Well, I do," she said. "And I should think you would, too!" Piers chewed stolidly, not looking at her. "Is that all you're going to say? And then go on eating?"

"I'm hungry."

"Well, I'm not. In fact, I lost my appetite practically the moment I came into this house!" Binky stopped, ashamed of this outburst. More quietly, she said, "Piers, what's wrong here? Your whole family—"

Now he did look at her, and for a moment his eyes were almost as hard as Karen's had been. Binky realized that this was the nearest she had ever come to seeing Piers angry. "My whole family *what?*"

She wanted to say that his father appeared to be an alcoholic, that his mother was weird (or maybe an alcoholic, too?), and that his sister was a mess. Instead, she drew a deep breath and said, "Okay, maybe it's none of my business. But you just don't want to think about any of it, do you? Much less talk about it."

"Right," Piers said.

Binky stood looking at him helplessly while he cleaned his plate and set it carefully on top of the mantel. He also opened a window a crack, a mannerism Binky was used to by now but still found irritating. Then, as if nothing had happened, as if Binky hadn't just been half shouting at him, he cleared his throat in a way that was all too familiar to her and said, "Ah . . . there's a new restaurant out on the way to Tucker Falls, supposed to be pretty good—big steaks, and all the salad you can eat. Brett and Doro thought they'd give it a try next weekend. You want to go along?"

Binky let herself take a last long look at his face—the rugged boy-man features, the heartrending blue clarity of the eyes, the firm mouth she'd once seen as sensitive and expressive. . . . "We can't even fight, can we?" she said sadly. "No, Piers, I don't want to go along next weekend. I don't like steak. Or rather, steak bores me."

You bore me, she wanted to say, but didn't, because after all, that wasn't his fault; and besides, in spite of everything, was it really quite true?

"And—well, I just don't really think we have very much in common, except . . . you know." She felt herself flushing a little, but lifted her chin and finished: "So I've been thinking we should cool it. Or—call it quits, actually."

He bowed his head, shoving his hands into his pockets. After a moment he said quietly, "And of course football season's over."

"That isn't the reason."

"Isn't it?" Their eyes met. He smiled slightly. "Part of it, anyway. . . . Oh, well, I suppose we were both just going along with the whole deal, and now—" He shrugged. "Who knows, maybe there's a basketball player in your future, Binky."

"Piers—"

"No hard feelings." He turned away, feeling in his pocket for car keys. "Come on, I'll take you home."

"No. You'd better stay here and—and help with the party," Binky said. Prop it up, she'd almost said. "I'll call my dad."

"Suit yourself."

He left the room, remembering to take the supper plates with him.

Slowly, Binky retrieved both of Karen's shoes and *To the Lighthouse* from the carpet and dropped them into the leather armchair. Then she looked around for the phone. It was the pushbutton kind, which she wasn't used to; besides which, she was suddenly and ridiculously half blinded by tears. She called two wrong numbers before she finally got her own.

8

After all, Binky decided, it was nice to be unattached again, to have time to spend with her family and with old friends she'd been neglecting lately—including Spencer, who greeted her return to the fold with a lack of surprise, which Binky, perversely, found rather irritating. Thanks to the lull between football and basketball seasons, she also had some leisure for painting and cooking and working out in her gym and just generally fooling around on her own. Sometimes she found herself wondering whether things might have been different with Piers if their practice schedules hadn't taken up so much time—if, instead of all those prearranged dates, they'd had some casual, ordinary time to spend together after school, and long Saturdays free of football games. . . .

But maybe not. Anyway, Piers was dating Heather Miles now. Binky told herself she ought to be feeling pleased at this confirmation of her matchmaking instincts. Certainly they made a good-looking couple, from the few glimpses she had of them together. She was just as glad the glimpses were few. She resolved not to get caught up again in the cheerleaders' social life once the basketball season began.

She did succeed in surprising Spencer on that score.

"You mean you're actually going on with this cheerleading bit? Come on, Binky—you've done your stint, proved your point, whatever. And what about the girl you replaced, Cathy what's-her-name? Isn't she healthy again? She probably wants her spot back."

"I don't think so," Binky told him. "Someone said she's into aerobics these days, or maybe it was weight-training. But even if she did—well, we're a team now. And Miss Walker—"

"Forget Miss Walker," Spencer said testily. "She doesn't own you. And what's with this team mentality bit? Good grief, Binky, you of all people."

"Well, I do feel some responsibility to the rest of them. But that's not the main reason," she went on, before Spencer could tell her she'd been brainwashed. "The thing is, I enjoy it. I like the exercise, and the excitement. In fact, I *like* being part of a team. And even more than that—well, this may come as a shock to you, Spencer, but you know what?" She grinned into his skeptical face. "I also like the feeling of power. Little me, Binky Nolan, turning on the crowd. You should understand about that."

Spencer groaned and put his head in his hands. "Good grief, what kind of monster have I created?" But when he looked up, his eyes were gleaming with amused speculation. "Ah, well. In that case, maybe it's time for some more headlines . . . you know, like that interview I promised you."

"Threatened me with, you mean. But sure, Spencer," Binky said blithely. "Anytime."

There was one aspect of the next stage in her cheerleading career that did give Binky pause—the new outfits they had to wear for performing in a heated gym. The skirt was a lightweight version of the football skirt (and just as red), but the white top . . . well, it was really nothing more than a tank top, the kind of thing Binky might wear around the house on a summer day; but to wear it in public—

"Dennis," Binky said one day at the start of Christmas vacation, "I need your opinion. I know my being a cheerleader embarrasses you anyway, and I'm sorry about that" —actually, Dennis had been a lot easier to live with since she'd broken up with Piers—"but this . . . do you think *other* people will be embarrassed?"

She posed in front of him nervously. She'd gone out and bought the tightest, firmest sports bra she could find, but even so—

Dennis eyed her judiciously. At least he wasn't blushing, Binky thought. "Well, you'll get lots of whistles," he said matter-of-factly. "Jump up and down." Binky did. "No, really jump, the way you would if—well, if we came from behind and tied the game with a minute to go." Binky jumped again; now it was she who was blushing. But Dennis said, "It's okay. You don't . . . wobble, or anything. Anyway, cheerleaders are supposed to be good-looking. If you happen to have a great figure, well, I don't think it's anything to be embarrassed about."

Binky stared at him. Was Dennis growing up? Or was it just that he liked basketball almost as much as he loathed football?

"Well, thanks," she said, though her feelings about her appearance were, if anything, more mixed than before. "At least we don't have to wear saddle shoes anymore, just sneakers."

She shivered—it was snowing outside—and turned to go change back into her sweater and jeans. Then it occurred to her that this might be a good time to mention something else she'd had on her mind. As casually as she could, she said, "Did you hear what the school play's going to be this year? *Cyrano de Bergerac.* I thought maybe—I wondered if —what I mean is, have you thought about trying out for it, Dennis? I bet you'd be a good actor. Or of course you could do something backstage," she added quickly.

But Dennis wasn't the least disconcerted. "Yeah," he said. "I wouldn't try out for Cyrano, though. I mean, I think I could *do* it okay, but they'd never give the lead to a freshman. So maybe I'll try out for Christian. That's the guy Roxane thinks she's in love with—sort of a jerk, but any- way. . . . And there're some minor parts that aren't too bad, some dukes and counts and things." Obviously he'd already been studying the play on his own. "I know I need experience," he added, with belated modesty.

As he sauntered away, Binky could almost see the sword clanking at his side. She noticed that he was no longer hunching his shoulders but standing tall. Well, soccer sea- son was over, she thought. Among other things. . . .

The day after Christmas, Sue Streibeck called with vari- ous news items, one of which was the fact that Piers and Heather had broken up. "Well, actually they only dated a few times," she said, "so I guess you couldn't really call it breaking up. He just stopped calling her. Poor Heather. . . . But anyway," Sue went on brightly, never one to brood on other people's woes, "I wouldn't be surprised if he called *you,* Binky. I mean, you two always seemed so right for each other."

She was fishing, Binky knew, since Binky had refused to offer any explanation as to why she and Piers had parted company (aside from anything else, it would have been hard to put into so many words). She said rather tartly, "Well, *I* would be—surprised, I mean. Do me a favor, Sue, and just forget it, will you?"

She meant it; and so when Piers phoned a few days later, it took her a moment to recognize his voice (or maybe to let herself recognize it), and longer to register what he was saying. A ski weekend in Vermont, organized by Tuck Zeller, whose uncle had a vacation house near Stowe; it wouldn't cost anything except food and gas and their tow tickets.

"A whole bunch of people are going, so it's not like a date or anything. I mean, you wouldn't be going with *me,*" Piers explained stiffly. "I just thought since you've never really skied before, this would be a good chance to learn. You'd have a couple of days, which makes a lot of difference when you're a beginner." When Binky was silent, he said, "Of course, it'll be over New Year's. Maybe you have other plans."

"No," Binky said, clutching the receiver against the swoop of her heart—clutching it, too, as if it could somehow tether her against an actual swoop down a vertical mountainside. "It's nice of you to think of me, Piers, but . . . well, I have this frostbite problem with my feet, like I told you, and—"

"You could wear extra socks. And warm up in the lodge between runs, if it got bad."

"I—no, I don't think so, Piers. It just wouldn't be much fun for me," Binky said, biting her lip at the understatement. "But I really appreciate your asking me. . . . I hope you have a good time."

"Sure," he said tonelessly. "Well, see you."

As luck would have it, he did see her—the very next morning, ice-skating on Jennings Pond.

Binky adored skating, and sometimes wished she'd started young, with regular lessons, instead of going in for gymnastics. She thought she might have been quite good.

But then, figure-skating would have been an even weirder
life than gymnastics, assuming she'd gone on with it—even
more travel and expense, to say nothing of all those chilly
practice hours in indoor rinks with her toes aching and
burning. . . .

They ached now, as they always did, but Binky was used
to the feeling, and it was a glorious morning on the pond—
very cold but sunny, and still early enough so that she had
the ice to herself except for some kids playing hockey at the
far end. She glided and twirled and tried a few jumps, copy-
ing what she'd seen figure skaters do on TV. Then, coming a
bit dizzily out of a spin, she saw a car slow down and stop
on the road that ran alongside the pond: a glossy red late-
model sedan . . . a Lincoln, in fact. Other people drove
Lincolns, of course, Binky told herself. She couldn't really
see the driver's face, only that he had straight blond hair;
that he was sitting very still; that he was staring at her.

The thermometer had read twenty-four degrees when
Binky left the house with her skates. She didn't need to be
told what Piers was thinking. She thought of stamping her
feet, of bending down to massage her toes, of skating
quickly over to the log at the side of the pond and unlacing
her skates as if the pain had suddenly grown too much for
her. . . . But it was too late. She'd lied, and now Piers
knew it.

She stared back at the car as if she could actually see the
accusation—and anger? disappointment?—in his eyes.
Then, defiantly, she turned her back and pushed off into a
figure eight. She hoped he couldn't see how shaky it was.
But when she looked again, the Lincoln was gone. Binky
felt cold now, as if all the warmth had gone from the sun.
But she forced herself to stay out on the ice for another half
hour, telling herself that Piers Anderssen meant nothing to
her anymore; certainly not enough to spoil the pleasure

she'd always taken—would continue to take, damn it—in ice-skating.

Basketball cheerleading turned out to be quite different from cheerleading at football games, Binky discovered, not only because they were indoors—and pretty hot and steamy it got, too, so that she was glad of her tank top and soon forgot her self-consciousness—but also because there was so little floor space. This limited their routines drastically; and although they weren't quite reduced to being pom-pom girls, their role was mostly confined to leading cheers during time-outs. Of course, they jumped up and down whenever Cameron scored a basket—but so did everybody else, the excitement level being considerably higher, Binky found, than at football games. There was also the fact that the cheerleaders had to freeze into immobility the instant play resumed, which sometimes meant kneeling uncomfortably for minutes at a time.

But this also meant that they got to watch the action close up—and far from being bored, Binky found herself enthralled by the speed and grace and intricacy of the game. Being short, she'd never had much to do with basketball; but the rules seemed simplicity themselves compared to football rules, and she soon developed an eye for the various patterns and set plays. She also developed an eagle eye for fouls, and sometimes had to be restrained by her fellow cheerleaders from rushing onto the court to protest a charging call that was clearly defensive interference, or a blocked shot that had been called goal-tending by a referee who was obviously nearsighted to the point of being legally blind.

"I never heard of their calling a technical because of a cheerleader," Miss Walker observed drily on one of these occasions, "but I suppose it could happen." Then, of course, she had to explain to Binky what a technical was—after which she added to the others, "It's just as well we don't cheerlead at baseball games. By the time Binky got through calling balls and strikes, she'd probably have the whole team thrown off the field."

There was one player Binky particularly admired, a short dark-haired guard named Pete Singer who could dribble circles around everyone else and who played full out in every game, not scoring much but setting up plays and making lightning-quick steals that left his opponents flatfooted and gaping. He was just the kind of player Binky felt she herself would have been if she'd played basketball.

Maybe Pete noticed her eyes on him, or shared the sense of affinity. Anyway, the admiration seemed to be mutual. But when he asked Binky for a date, she refused.

"But why?" Sue demanded. "He's a nice guy, you'd like him. And you'd make a really cute couple—you know?"

Cute couple, super couple . . . Binky'd had enough of that kind of thing. She'd also had enough of supposing that how a person performed on the playing field—or basketball court—had anything to do with what he was like off it. For all she knew, Pete Singer spent his free time watching bowling on TV.

Besides, Piers' remark about the basketball player in her future still stung.

She almost weakened when she learned that Piers was now dating Melissa Grant—"heavy dating," someone said with a smirk. Cat-eyed, spiteful, pretty Melissa, with her razor-sharp mind and a tongue that went with it . . . it was all too easy to imagine what she saw in Piers. Certainly it wasn't his witty conversation.

Binky said no again to Pete; but feeling maybe there was a vacuum in her life that needed filling, began going out with Ted Fiske, the erstwhile place kicker, who fortunately wasn't the least bit interested in talking about football. Ted was a pleasant, undemanding companion with varied interests the chief of which was architecture—his father was an architect, and Ted hoped to become one, too. They spent a lot of time on weekends driving around looking at buildings. Cameron, being an old New England town, had its share of seventeenth- and eighteenth-century houses; nearby Livingston, which had been burned during the Revolution, was mostly Victorian. Binky learned a lot about pediments and bays and roof lines. Often she took her sketch pad along— she'd enrolled in the art class Dennis had told her about, and it was a good chance to practice what she was learning about perspective.

Once she showed Ted the Spragues' southern mansion; he studied it for an incredulous moment and then burst out laughing. Although Binky laughed, too, she felt an odd little pang, as though she'd betrayed someone or something. After all, people were entitled to their dreams, no matter how absurd they might look from the outside.

The Fiskes themselves lived in an angular modern house which Ted's father had designed—the kind of house which should have been stark and uncluttered inside but which instead was pleasantly overrun by Ted's four younger brothers and sisters and a fluctuating number of dogs; Mrs. Fiske was addicted to taking in strays. Binky enjoyed the whole family, and spent more time there than she probably should have, except that she was always made to feel welcome.

"They're—well, they're our kind of people," she explained to her mother. "I just feel at home there."

"Besides which, Mrs. Fiske is probably a better cook than I am," Liz teased her. But she looked at Binky thoughtfully. "I hope you're not turning into a snob, Binky. Well, no, that's not really what I mean," she said hastily as Binky opened her mouth in outrage. "It's just that you have such definite ideas about things, especially people, and—well, you do have a tendency to be a bit inflexible at times."

"If you mean about Piers' family—" Binky began hotly. But apparently Liz didn't. Instead, she was off on one of her tangents. "Maybe it's because you're a graphic artist—you know, surfaces, two dimensions. Whereas a sculptor . . ." Her face took on its abstracted look; Binky figured she was thinking about her latest creation out in the workshop, a tottering six-foot metal figure that looked to Binky like nothing so much as the Tin Woodman. They were all afraid it would fall over on top of Liz one day.

"By the way," Liz said, returning her attention to Binky, "I love the house sketches you've been doing, Binky. *Much* better than photographs for getting across the feel of a place. I wonder if the real estate people will ever realize that . . . well, I guess they'd better not, or I'd be out of business. Now, what was I saying? Oh, yes, about Ted." She fixed her daughter with a penetrating stare.

"Ted's family," Binky corrected.

"No, Ted himself. All his family is doing is confusing the issue," her mother said firmly. "He's crazy about you, do you realize that?"

"Oh, Mom! Crazy—Ted?"

"Well, maybe that's putting it too strongly, but anyway, a lot more interested in you than I suspect you are in him."

"I—we're just good friends," Binky said uncomfortably, remembering the number of times recently when she'd had to edge away from what threatened to be more than a simple good-night kiss. It was true, she wasn't attracted to Ted in that way. But—

"Enough said, I trust," said Liz, who'd been watching her face.

But. Fuming at her mother, Binky thought things over, saw her point, and reluctantly began seeing less of Ted. It wasn't long before he got the message, swallowed whatever disappointment he might have felt, and took up again with Vicky Mottram, a former girlfriend who still had a thing for Ted—but who, Binky knew, was just a nice kid as far as Ted was concerned.

Why can't things be better organized? Binky wondered mournfully. Why can't the person who's entertaining and interesting and easy to be with also be the person who sets off little colored rockets inside your head? And vice-versa?

The Cameron basketball team was doing far better than anyone had expected. By the beginning of March it looked as if they might have a chance at the conference play-offs; and cheerleading at the games was no longer the simple, pleasurable job it had been, at least not at the home games. Suddenly it had become the thing to do to show up at the gym on Friday nights; and "crowd control," as Binky continued to think of it, became a real concern.

In fact, Binky was beginning to find the whole scene a bit scary—the gym packed to the rafters, rocking and reverberating in a continuous pandemonium from the starting whistle to the final buzzer. There was a lion's-den feeling about being down on the lighted floor, caged in by all the screaming people. Fights began breaking out in the parking lot afterward; and as the hysteria mounted, there was no nonsense about not using cops—they were stationed not only at the exits but in the stands.

The "element" began turning out in full force, choosing as usual to occupy a top row, and still wearing their black leather gear in spite of the heat, which must have been considerable way up there under the ceiling. Binky identified Karen Anderssen among them, looking thinner and sulkier than ever, but also more nervous, almost twitchy, as if— Binky thought worriedly—she might be "on" something.

This was in contrast to her friends, most of whom had the slack, sloppy manner of people who'd been drinking.

At school Binky sometimes encountered Karen in the halls, and once or twice had tried to speak to her, but Karen simply stared right through her. (Piers, at least, always nodded and said hello; distantly, coldly.) The Monday after one of the home games, feeling somehow haunted by the girl—even responsible for her somehow, which was ridiculous—Binky asked Adrienne Frank about Karen in chemistry lab.

"I never did really get to know her when I was going out with Piers," she said—which was putting it mildly. "But she doesn't look too good to me."

Adrienne shrugged. "I never even see her anymore, to talk to. All I know is, she's absent a lot of the time, or late when she does come to school. And I don't think she ever does any homework. But I don't think she's sick or anything."

Well, that depended on your definition of "sick," Binky thought, feeling a little sick herself. Her one encounter with Karen had left her in no doubt about the girl's intelligence; and she did have one thing going for her—her interest in writing. Binky remembered guiltily that she never had spoken to Spencer about Karen. Tryouts for the paper would be coming up soon. . . . But was what Karen Anderssen did or didn't do with her life really any concern of hers?

Somehow, Binky discovered on Friday night, it was.

The game was an important one for Cameron. If they lost, they'd still have one more chance to make the play-offs, but that would be an away game without the home-court advantage. Binky began having that lion's-den feeling again as the gym filled up until there was standing-room only, but she supposed it *was* an advantage for the team. At least, they played brilliantly during the first half, ending it with a ten-point lead.

During the break there was a foul-shooting competition, and little for the cheerleaders to do until the teams came back on the floor. People were milling about excitedly in the stands, with fewer than usual leaving their seats to go outside for a breath of fresh air.

Or a breath of something else. "There go the troops," Caroline said to Binky, nodding toward one of the exits. "Let's just hope they all pass out during the second half." Binky caught a glimpse of black jackets, and recognized the back of Bobby Gerard's greasy head; also Karen's blond one. "Cindy Brandt's in some kind of weird mood," Caroline explained. "I've been watching her. If she has another drink or two out there . . ." She shook her head.

"But don't the cops check people when they come back in?"

"I guess they try to, but with this mob . . . Besides, that crew probably spends as much on breath mints as they do on cheap Scotch," Caroline said cynically. "Anyway, better keep an eye on them."

When play resumed, it looked at first as if Cameron would walk away with the game. The team scored six unanswered points, and the crowd went wild. Then there was one of those letups Binky had learned to expect. The Cameron players began stalling, playing the clock (much too soon, Binky thought critically, with her newfound expertise), passing the ball around without trying for the basket. The passes became softer and sloppier. There was one steal, then another. Trying belatedly to regain momentum, Cameron began overplaying, committing fouls that even Binky couldn't question. With eight minutes left in the game the Cameron lead had shrunk to three points, and now the team was playing scared, Binky realized, afraid of getting into worse foul trouble.

Then Pete Singer, who'd been taken out for a rest, came

back onto the floor. He was charged up, or at least putting on a good act, obviously trying to psych his teammates back into some aggressive play. If anyone could do it, Pete could, Binky thought, watching appreciatively as he intercepted a pass and went thundering down the court for a layup—more of a dink than a dunk, given Pete's small stature, but still a solid two points for Cameron.

"Little Pete! Little Pete!" yelled the crowd.

"Go, Wizards, go!" yelled the cheerleaders, shaking their red-and-white pom-poms in unison.

On the next play Pete tried another steal. This time he was tripped, deliberately, and went down hard, smashing onto the floorboards with a *smack* Binky could hear even above the noise of the crowd. She cringed as Pete rolled over, holding his shoulder. The trainer came running out onto the court, an injury time-out was called. The crowd was hushed, watching as the trainer felt Pete's arm and shoulder, watching Pete bite his lip and close his eyes against the pain.

Then, from high up in the stands, a girl's voice screamed shrilly, "You dirty little slut! I'm going to fix you! You just wait. When I get finished with you—"

The rest of the words were lost in the sounds of a scuffle —grunts and curses, a cry of pain. All eyes turned to the end of a topmost row, where Cindy Brandt, her face contorted with rage under her black cap, was apparently trying to scratch out Karen Anderssen's eyes. Bobby Gerard, swaying and giggling between them, was making a half-hearted effort to hold the two girls apart.

There was only the single railing between Karen and a very long drop to the floor, Binky noted, her mind beginning to work furiously, and if Cindy lunged again . . . But now a cop was moving in on them swiftly, he had Cindy by the arm—

"Quick," Binky said to the cheerleaders. "The Swallow Dive."

"The Swallow Dive—Binky, that's too dangerous to do here, on a hard floor." Doro stared at her.

"Lynette, Caroline, come on," Binky said urgently. "Heather, you help me with the mount."

Cindy Brandt was struggling with the cop, cursing and snarling; Karen was crying, her hands over her face. Another cop was advancing toward them.

Binky vaulted into position.

The first cop was hustling Cindy down the steps. The other had Karen by the arm. She was clinging to the railing with her free hand; he pried it loose. In another moment, Binky saw, he would be escorting Karen down through the bleachers into the glaring lights of the gym floor, crossing long yards of empty space to the exit—

Binky clapped her hands. "One, two, three, four, *five!*" she yelled, and took off.

She was never quite sure afterward just what went wrong. Abby insisted tearfully that it had been her fault, that she hadn't gotten braced in time; but Binky thought her own timing might have been off by a fraction of a second.

All she knew at the moment was that she was off balance going into the second flip, that she wasn't going to make it, that there was no time to roll into the fall and take it on her shoulder. Instead, she stuck out her right arm to break the impact—and as she landed, felt something snap, in the instant before pinwheels of pain exploded in front of her eyes and she fainted.

Binky sat on a green plastic couch in the emergency waiting room of Livingston Hospital. Her broken wrist had been set and encased in a cast that ran from her knuckles to above her elbow, and they'd given her something for the pain. Caroline, who'd driven her to the hospital, had gone off to the pay phone to call Binky's parents and Miss Walker.

People came and went, some of them looking curiously at Binky in her skimpy cheerleader's outfit. Binky didn't mind that. She only wished she didn't feel so cold. Everyone else arrived in jackets or coats, which they stripped off after a while. In fact, there was a pile of them on the chair next to her. Binky thought of asking someone if she could borrow a jacket for a few minutes, just to put around her shoulders, but it seemed like too much effort. Better, anyway, to concentrate on how cold she felt than to think about her wrist and the weeks that would have to go by before she could use a paintbrush again, or a stick of charcoal, or even a soft-leaded art pencil—

An unlikely trio entered the waiting room. Binky blinked, trying to focus her eyes. Her brother, Dennis; Piers Anderssen; Karen Anderssen. Karen had a gauze patch over one eyebrow, and the long scratches on her cheeks were garish with antiseptic. Her lower lip was swollen. She stared at Binky, attempted a sardonic smile, and began to tremble. Piers put his arm around her, led her over to the green couch, and pushed her down gently next to Binky. She turned her head aside, but Binky saw that she was crying.

"Broken?" Piers said, looking down at Binky's cast. A man of few words, Binky remembered, and tried to smile. If only she didn't feel so groggy. That must be the effect of the pain-killer.

"My wrist," she said. "I know it looks like my whole arm, but it's just my wrist. I don't know why they had to put this monster cast on it."

"Oh, my gosh, Binky, it's your *right* wrist, isn't it?" Dennis said, finding his tongue at last. He looked almost as pale and shocked as Karen. "Of all the crazy things to do. I couldn't believe it when I saw you on top of that pyramid."

Binky had forgotten that Dennis had been at the game. "What are you doing here?" she asked stupidly. "I mean, how did you get here?"

"Piers gave me a ride. We were both—well, we sort of joined forces," Dennis said, with an embarrassed look at Karen.

Then Piers had been at the game, too, Binky thought, trying to make sense of things. With Melissa Grant, probably. What had he done with Melissa? Well, never mind that now. "How's Pete?" she asked. When they looked at her blankly, she said, "Pete Singer. The third casualty, you might say."

"He's okay," Caroline said, joining them. "He had to sit out the rest of the game, but he'll be able to play next week, or in the play-offs, anyway. We won," she explained; and added, looking at their faces, "If anyone cares. I got hold of your parents, Binky," she went on briskly. "They wanted to come get you, but I said I'd take you home. And here's the prescription from the pharmacy. I thought I might as well get it filled here."

"Thanks, Caroline," Binky said. "You've been really great." She noticed enviously that Caroline was wearing a coat over her cheerleader's uniform. Someone had wrapped a blanket around her for the ride to the hospital, she remembered now; it must still be in Caroline's car. She shivered, taking the bottle of pills, and squinted at the label. "I don't know, though—these pills are awfully strong. Maybe just aspirin. . . ."

"I broke my wrist once," Caroline told her grimly. "You'll need them."

Piers had seen the shiver. He took off his Cameron jacket and put it around Binky's shoulders, careful not to touch the cast. Then he turned to Caroline. "I'll take Binky home. It's more on my way than it is on yours."

"Well . . ." Caroline hesitated, her eyes flickering from Binky to Piers. She'd been avoiding looking at Karen, Binky noticed. "Okay, maybe that would be best. Especially if you're driving one of those big squashy cars—easier on broken bones than my old VW. I practically fracture my spine every time I hit a pothole." When only Binky smiled, she shrugged and said, "Well, I guess I'll be on my way, then. Take care, Binky. Everyone'll be thinking of you. In fact, Miss Walker sends her love . . . how *about* that?" She flashed Binky a smile and left.

"I think Miss Walker should be cursing you out," Dennis muttered. "Talk about fractured spines—you could have broken your back, do you realize? I still don't see why you had to go and do such a dumb thing."

There was an awkward little silence. Karen stirred, but didn't say anything.

"Well, at least I won't be cheerleading anymore this year, Dennis," Binky said as lightly as she could. "That ought to make you happy."

Piers said quietly, "Binky was trying to take people's attention away from my sister, Dennis." He gave a short laugh. "It worked, that's for sure." As Dennis gaped at him, he said, "Come on, let's go get the car. I had to park about half a mile away," he explained to Binky, "so it'll take us a while." He held her gaze for a moment—Binky had forgotten just how blue his eyes were—and nodded almost imperceptibly at Karen's huddled figure.

Oh, no, Binky thought, I can't handle this; not another cozy little talk with Karen, not now. She looked around the waiting room, empty now except for an elderly man reading a newspaper across the way, and closed her eyes for a moment. Her wrist throbbed.

But unexpectedly it was Karen who spoke first. "Does it hurt a lot?" she asked in a muffled voice. "No, stupid question. What I really want to know is . . . was it true, what Piers said?"

Now, finally, she turned to look at Binky, who winced inwardly at the sight of her disfigured face. But although Karen's eyes were reddened and swollen from crying, their gaze was direct and unflinching. This was someone you didn't lie to. So she said, "Yes. I don't know what happened between you and that Cindy character, but it was getting to be sort of a production, what with the cops and all, and I didn't think anyone needed that. So I decided to—well, provide a distraction."

"Defending the honor of Cameron High, I suppose? Or . . . or Piers' honor?" Karen's attempt at sarcasm was more pathetic than anything else, as she herself seemed to realize. She looked down, playing with the zipper of her black jacket with thin fingers that shook a little.

"I think I was mainly thinking of you," Binky said, honestly trying to analyze her own motives. "I guess I just didn't think you belonged in that kind of scene. I could see Cindy was drunk, and—well, whatever it looked like, you're not that kind of person."

"Aren't I?" Karen laughed harshly. "Look at me, with the scars to prove it."

"No."

Karen turned her face away again. After a moment she pulled a tissue from her pocket and blew her nose. "Well, thanks for that," she said, and drew a deep breath. "I guess tonight was really rock bottom. Now there's nowhere to go but up. If only I could figure out which way was up."

"Your writing?" Binky said tentatively, and waited for Karen to lash out at her. But she didn't. "And I'm sure there are lots of other things, Karen . . . lots of other people, for instance."

Karen was silent for a moment. Then she said tiredly, "Other people, that's for sure. You're right, Cindy was drunk, not that that's anything new, and so were the rest of them. They were always trying to get me to drink with them, but I wouldn't   I hate the taste of the stuff. And then tonight, Bobby Gerard . . ."

She stopped, hunching over again with her face in her hands. Binky waited.

"He and Cindy are always fighting about something; in fact they had a big fight before the game tonight. And then, after he'd had a few drinks, he started pawing me." She shuddered. "Ugh, that creep—I couldn't stand to have him touch me, but I didn't know what to do, I didn't want to make a big scene. . . ." She gave a miserable, choked little laugh that wasn't quite a sob. "Then all of a sudden Cindy just freaked out. She said I was trying to take Bobby away from her, and she started calling me all these names—well, I guess you heard that part of it. I guess everyone did. And then . . . she just *went* for me. It was horrible."

Awkwardly, Binky put her good arm around Karen's shoulders, feeling how painfully thin and tense she was. "It's all over now," she said. "You don't have to have anything to do with them ever again. And as far as people at the game are concerned—well, I don't think most of them could even see what was going on. Or if they did, they couldn't really see who was involved. It was pretty shadowy way up in that corner."

"Do you think so?" Binky could feel Karen's body begin to relax a little. "When that cop started trying to drag me down out of the stands—I didn't know whether he was going to arrest me or what, but I didn't care about that, all I could think of was that then everybody *would* see . . . and they would've, except for you. And when I think how I've hated you all this time. . . ."

She was crying again, but this time Binky could feel that the tears were a release, a way of letting go.

"I'm sorry about that." Karen gulped. "About hating you, I mean. It wasn't just because of Piers, it was—oh, just the way you were so cute and popular and sure of yourself. The old green-eyed monster, I guess. And now . . . now you turn out to be *nice,* too. It's almost too much!" she wailed.

A family came into the waiting room. The smallest child, a little boy, wandered over to where Binky sat with her arm around Karen and stood staring at them. "What'd she do to her face?" he inquired with interest.

"She—she had an accident," Binky said, managing a smile.

"Oh." The child nodded knowledgeably. "And so did

you," he said, looking at Binky's cast. "And so did Mommy, she burned her hand. That's why we had to come to the hospital," he added importantly. Pleased with this summary of events, he went back to his family.

Karen, belatedly aware of an audience, sat up now and blew her nose again. "An accident," she said, with a watery smile. "Well, that's one way of putting it."

Binky withdrew her arm and used her free hand to prop her cast into a more comfortable position. "Maybe that's the way you *should* think of it," she told Karen thoughtfully. "Like everything that's happened since you came to Cameron has been a sort of accident, and now . . . They're holding tryouts for the paper next week, you know."

"Oh, the paper." But Karen sat still, obviously thinking about it.

Binky shifted position again, knocked her cast against the arm of the couch by mistake, and said, "Ow!" before she could stop herself.

Karen looked down at what could be seen of Binky's right hand. "Will you be able to write with that thing on? Do homework and stuff, I mean?"

Binky flexed her fingers, and then was sorry she had. "I guess after a few days . . . and in a week or so they'll put on a smaller cast. But painting—well, I guess that's out for a while."

"Painting?" Karen stared at her. "You're an artist?"

"Well, most people probably wouldn't think so," Binky told her. "I'm mainly interested in illustrating. Nature subjects, mostly—you know, flowers and trees, maybe birds and insects when I get good enough. Although I've been getting interested in architecture too, lately. . . ." Why was she talking so much about her painting, something she normally never did? It must be the pills. In fact, Binky was beginning to feel distinctly sleepy. She yawned, and finished: "What I'd like to do eventually is illustrate textbooks or field guides or maybe children's books about nature . . . you know."

"Nature," Karen repeated, and gave Binky an odd look. "But Piers—"

Whatever she was going to say was interrupted by the return of Piers himself, tall and glowing, bringing with him a welcome breath of fresh night air, of health, of life going on as usual. Suddenly Binky could hardly wait to get out of this place. He looked swiftly at Karen, and seemed satisfied with what he saw.

"Come on," he said. "I'm in a no-parking zone now, and Dennis is holding the fort." He helped Binky to her feet. Karen preceded them into the lobby and out the automatic doors. Binky looked up at Piers and—feeling a flash of her old exasperation—answered the question she knew he wouldn't ask.

"I think she'll be okay now," she said. "Whatever it was, I think she's got it out of her system—not just tonight, I mean, but that whole bad scene. The only thing is"—she hesitated—"is Karen on something, do you think? I mean, I know she doesn't drink, but the way she's so thin and nervous—"

"I'm sure she isn't," Piers said. "I don't think she's been sleeping much, and lately she's hardly eaten anything, but I'm pretty sure that's just nerves. Like inside she's been wanting to break away from that crowd and get herself together, but she didn't know how to go about it. And then being pressured about it at home . . ." He pondered a moment. "I guess maybe I came on too strong sometimes. Karen's pretty stubborn, and she also has—well, her own kind of pride, even when she knows she's in the wrong."

It was the longest speech Binky had ever heard Piers make, and in a way the most personal.

"I guess that's true of us all," she said. He did care, she thought. Of course he cared, all along. He just couldn't talk about it. "Piers—"

But she didn't really quite know what she wanted to say to Piers, and anyway, they were almost at the car. It was a silver Lincoln like the one Piers had driven on their first date. But probably not the same one, she thought, with an odd little pang; it would be a later model.

Karen had already gotten into the car with Dennis. Piers stopped a few feet short of it and put a hand on Binky's shoulder, turning her to face him. "I just want to say thanks a whole lot, Binky," he said, looking down at her somberly. "I'm sorry it had to turn out the way it did for you."

"Oh"—Binky managed a grin and a shrug—"you know me. Just a clumsy type."

A uniformed hospital guard came up behind them. "Okay, kids, move it," he said, with an impatient jerk of his head. "You can play this scene someplace else, where you're not blocking traffic."

They weren't, as far as Binky could see, but they got into the Lincoln obediently. She'd been right: this one had crimson upholstery, and it was leather, not plush—not the same car at all.

"Seen any more of Piers?" Dennis inquired a week or so later, watching Binky shake some tarragon into the chicken casserole their mother had left simmering on the stove for dinner. She would have liked to add some chopped onion, too, but still hadn't mastered the use of a knife with her left hand. Not being able to cook was almost as frustrating as not being able to paint.

"Just around," Binky said, adding a dash of pepper.

She'd hoped—well, she didn't know just what she'd hoped.
At least she didn't see Piers around with Melissa Grant
anymore. And he didn't seem to be dating anyone new.
"Why?"

"Oh . . . just he's a nicer guy than I thought," Dennis
said, in a jaunty tone that didn't quite conceal a note of
apology. "I'm sorry if I gave you a hard time about him,
Bink."

"That's okay."

"I mean—well, I hope it wasn't part of the reason you
two broke up."

Binky wheeled around to stare at Dennis, who was leaning against a counter with his arms folded, gazing into space
with a melancholy air. He'd grown not only taller but
broader in the shoulders over the past few months, Binky
observed. She also observed that his hair was freshly cut
and that his new sage-green sweater matched the green
flecks in his hazel eyes.

"Dennis, I hate to tell you, but the world doesn't revolve
around you, even if you did get the second lead in *Cyrano*."
For to his parents' astonishment, Dennis had tried out successfully for the part of Christian. The play was now in
rehearsal, and although Dennis wasn't quite taking fencing
lessons, he was being coached in the deployment of a plastic
sword. "And stop *posing,* will you?" Binky added, suppressing a smile.

Dennis stiffened, decided not to be offended, and relaxed.
"This whole family is really coming out of the closet, you
know? Me with my acting"—he put the words in capitals—
"and Mom selling one of her things. . . . The guy must be
slightly nuts, though, don't you think, to pay all that money
for it? And where's he going to put the thing, anyway?"

The "thing" was the Tin Woodman sculpture, bought by
one of the realtors Liz worked for. He'd come to the house

to check a brochure layout and had, as Liz put it, surprised her in the act, leather apron and all; after which (he was a youngish man with what he described importantly as "eclectic tastes") he'd gone into ecstasies over the contents of the workshop. Nothing would do for his own collection but the largest piece of them all—a lucky choice from Liz's point of view, since the Tin Woodman was taking up valuable space, and also from her family's, since they considered it a menace.

"And then there's your exhibit," Dennis went on.

"Oh, Dennis, it isn't really an exhibit," Binky said. "Just one wall of one room of the library. Probably no one will even notice it."

Because of her broken wrist, her art teacher had suggested that Binky spend some class time putting together a portfolio of work she'd already done—spraying fixative on drawings and sketches, mounting her watercolors. She'd brought in one of her flower series—the studies of white wildflowers—and he'd liked them so much that he'd arranged display space for them in the public library downtown. He'd even lettered an elegant narrow placard to go above them: "Watercolors by Rosemary Nolan." Binky had hesitated for some time between "Bianca" and "Rosemary," and finally decided that Rosemary went better with her kind of painting. Besides, it would please her father.

Thinking of her father, she began to laugh. "I don't think you could say Dad came out of the closet, exactly," she said. "More like shot from a cannon."

"Yeah." Dennis grinned, and then shook his head. "It's a good thing Mr. Fuller has a sense of humor. Or maybe he's just crazy, like Dad is. I mean, the way it sounds, Dad could have *killed* the guy."

Mr. Fuller was a senior vice-president of their father's company, encountered—or rather, smashed into—by Gerald last weekend while they were both whitewater-canoeing in the wilds of New Hampshire. According to Gerald, he'd taken a slight risk in shooting a certain rapids, had lost his paddle, and had caromed into another canoe at the bottom, slamming it against some rocks and opening a large hole in its side. Even when the spray had cleared and the occupants had established that neither was hurt, it took them some time to recognize each other, since neither had ever seen the other in anything but a three-piece business suit. They had already made plans for another whitewater expedition later in the spring, this time in kayaks. "At least the funeral will be a nice company affair," was Liz's comment.

April had arrived and was deciding whether to stay or go —sleet one day, then sunshine, then two inches of snow— when Binky learned that yet another person had come out of the closet, as Dennis put it: Karen Anderssen.

"Hey," said Spencer, accosting Binky outside the cafeteria one day, "why didn't you tell me about this Anderssen kid? She's a natural for the paper. In fact, if she turns out as well as I think she will, I may even be putting her up for editor next year when it's time for me to hang up my typewriter and all my nasty blue pencils."

Binky still wasn't sure just how Spencer had managed to get himself named editor of the *Scroll* for two years running, when the usual term was one year, but she supposed this was a generous thought. Anyway, she was delighted for Karen. "Well, I didn't know if she was any good," she told Spencer—though the real reason she hadn't mentioned Karen to him was a superstitious feeling that unless Karen made the approach on her own, it wouldn't count, somehow. "I mean, I knew she wrote poetry—"

"Poetry," Spencer scoffed. "I bet it's terrible. No, she's a natural journalist—she sees, she observes, she gets the details, she writes down exactly what she sees. And can also slant the facts when necessary," he added, giving Binky an evil grin. "In short, she has the gimlet eye, unclouded by sentimentality. Just like yours truly, in fact."

"I'm glad to hear it," Binky said, but a bit uneasily; Spencer was regarding her with a certain intensity which, she knew from long experience, meant he was holding something back. "Okay, Spencer," she said. "What else? Why the gimlet eye on *me?*"

"Well"—he studied her thoughtfully, as if making up his mind about something—"for the tryouts this year, I asked everybody to write a character sketch. It could be of someone they knew well, or someone they didn't know at all, in which case they'd write pure description, make deductions, and so on. Good practice for feature writing. Most of them chose to write about someone they knew well."

"So?" Binky looked at him blankly.

"So Karen Anderssen's sketch was most interesting. Not only well written, but interesting in itself, once you figured out who the subject was, which wasn't hard. In fact, I'm thinking of printing it, under some such heading as 'Dr. Jekyll and the Jock.' I thought maybe you might like to read it."

"Yes," Binky said slowly. "I think maybe I would."

"Be my guest," Spencer said, leading the way to the *Scroll* office. Binky looked at her watch. She'd probably be late for her history class, but she had a feeling she'd better take Spencer up on his offer right now; something about his mood told her he was quite capable of withdrawing it.

In the office he handed her a manila folder with Karen's name on it. It contained various writing exercises, including headline writing and a lengthy quiz on how and by what means you would follow up a story about a four-year-old boy discovering a cache of stolen jewelry in a cranberry bog

—Spencer had clearly been enjoying putting the aspirants through their paces. The character sketch was at the back, a page of single-spaced typing, untitled. Binky sat down on a scarred wooden chair and began to read.

He is not what he seems. But then, which of us is? The world sees a strikingly good-looking boy, tall and athletic, with an athlete's air of self-containment. He moves and speaks with deliberation. He is polite and a bit remote. Is he intelligent? His grades say so, but of course he never speaks about his grades.

The more perceptive may suspect that he is really quite shy. But few realize that his public image is only a shell for a sensitive, talented, many-faceted individual.

People in the small midwestern town where he grew up knew him as an outdoor boy who spent all his free time exploring the woods and ponds and streams. They didn't know that his interest was not in fishing or hunting but in the lore of plants and animals and birds and fish. Nor did they know that he was becoming an accomplished wildlife photographer whose work had been published in a number of regional and national magazines by the time he was sixteen. They didn't know of his related interests in geology and paleontology, fields in which he has read extensively.

In his new town in semi-urban New England, people know him as a football star who dates pretty cheerleaders and likes to ski. If they think at all of his future, they assume that he will go on to a college where he can major in football, skiing, and cheerleaders while minoring in something safe and dull like economics or business administration. Instead, I think he will be exploring and testing himself, trying to decide between a variety of careers—in conservation, in zoology, in anthropology. He could become a naturalist, a forester, a teacher, a civil engineer.

He is honest to a fault, and will never say what other people want to hear unless it happens to be true. This accounts for his reserve in public life. With his family he is a different person—warm and caring, showing his awareness of their needs through a hundred small actions as much as in words. He also has a dry sense of humor, usually concealed by a poker face, which helps put things in perspective at times of crisis. In fact, this magazine-cover jock has been the glue that has held one family together during a difficult time in all their lives.

Binky stared at the last sentence—where Spencer had circled the word "glue" and written "poor image, besides being trite"—and felt her eyes filling with tears. She kept her head down so that Spencer wouldn't see. Carefully she replaced the sheet of paper in the folder.

Spencer said, "Am I right in assuming most of that was news to you?"

Binky nodded. She looked down at the folder in her lap and said in a low voice, "I never really knew him at all. Sometimes I thought there was more . . . but mostly I just saw the surface."

"Well, surfaces are easier to deal with," Spencer said matter-of-factly. "And let's face it, Bink, imagination has never been your strong suit."

That hurt. Binky looked up at Spencer, who was lounging

behind his desk in his usual editorial pose; but his face was as neutral as his tone had been.

"I guess not," she said at last. "But Spencer—why? Why the shell, I mean? Karen doesn't explain that."

He shrugged. "Probably only Piers could. Oh, I suppose we could talk about peer pressure and the way people tend to let themselves get typed, also about uptight Scandinavians. . . . But heck, Binky, everyone has their defenses—their shells. Even me," he said, with the air of someone making a damaging admission.

That made Binky smile. "Especially you," she said. "You're *all* shell, Spencer."

"Why, Binky," he said, pretending injury. Then he grinned. "A rather elegant one, if I do say so myself. . . . But what about you? For instance, how did you come across to Piers, do you think? Did you ever talk about anything that really mattered to you? Or did you just keep playing the cute, chatty little cheerleader—being entertaining for all you were worth?"

Binky thought back. A hollow feeling was growing inside her, as if—maybe psyched by Karen's metaphor—the person sitting here in her crisp yellow oxford-cloth shirt and denim skirt, her hair washed last night, her homework done, her teeth brushed both before and after breakfast— were only a fragile skin stretched tight over a big, confused, cloudy *ache*.

Blindly she replaced the folder on the desk. Spencer picked it up and riffled through the pages to the character sketch.

"Yes, some good stuff here," he said, scanning it. "I've been thinking we might run a kind of mystery series—'Can You Guess Who This Is?' Or call it something like 'Shadow Profiles,' with a subhead: 'How Much Do You Really Know About Your Fellow Students?'"

"Spencer, you wouldn't!"

"We could do a piece on you, for instance. I'd write that one, of course—Binky in the woods with her magnifying glass, on the trail of the purple-spotted bog lily. And Tom Perry's a good friend of Kevin Foreman, our computer genius, so I happen to know that Kevin's failed his driver's test twice and can barely remember his own phone number from one day to the next. Then, let's see—there's elegant, sophisticated Sharon Lounsbury, who's still carrying a torch for a total clod by the name of—"

"I don't want to know," Binky interrupted hotly. "Not everyone is willing to rat on their friends' private lives, Spencer. And as for that piece about Piers—it would kill him! To say nothing of what it would do to Karen. . . . You can't. You won't."

"Ah," said Spencer, waving the folder in the air, a glint in his eye. "I can see what's coming. That little blackmail threat about my book review experiment—right?" He studied Binky's face for a moment, and then relented, tipping his chair forward and replacing the folder on his desk.

"Just teasing, Bink. I admit it was something of a struggle, trying to decide between playing Cupid or going all out for Mephistopheles . . . but in the end, Cupid won."

"Cupid?" Binky drew an exasperated breath. "Spencer, you really are too much."

"Am I? Why else did I show you Karen's sketch? Come on, Binky, you've been eating your heart out for the guy all year long, whether you know it or not. Can't fool old Uncle Spencer. Who"—he studied his stubby ink-stained fingertips—"admits to a certain jealousy of handsome jocks, even the kind with wooden heads. As for this one . . . well, not such a mismatch after all, I guess, where you're concerned. Just thought you ought to know."

He cleared his throat. When he looked up, the glint was

back in his eye, the sardonic smile firmly in place. "Besides, I do feel kind of responsible, having, as you might say, engineered the match in the first place. The 'Supercouple' thing, I mean. Tom took the picture and did the layout, but I'm afraid the headline was my very own."

Binky stared at him wordlessly. Then she rose. "I'm glad Karen made the paper, Spencer," she said formally. "And now, if you'll excuse me, I'm late for history."

"You're never too late for history," was Spencer's parting shot. "As one who enjoys making it, I know."

10

"Piers?" Binky's hand on the receiver was almost as slippery with sweat as it had been the first time she'd called him, way back last fall. "This is Binky."

"I know." A pause. "How've you been?"

"Oh, fine."

It was like playing back an old tape. Next thing she knew, she'd be asking how *he* was, hearing that he, too, was fine, and thus arriving at the inevitable next pause. But no, she thought determinedly. Not this time; not anymore.

"Actually," she said, "my wrist still isn't quite healed, and I—well, I have a favor to ask of you. Or a couple of favors, really. I want to get out and do some painting tomorrow"—would Karen have told him about her painting? —in her present reckless mood Binky decided she didn't really care—"and even though I got my license a couple of weeks ago, my parents aren't too happy about my driving around on country roads, what with the potholes and all." Not exactly a lie; she did have trouble gripping the wheel, and if her parents *had* known about any such plan . . .

"Country roads."

"Piers," Binky said carefully, "I wish you wouldn't always repeat what I say. It's very irritating." And that, she thought, might be the end of the conversation right there. But she wasn't going to hold back anymore; she'd made her mind up about that during the long two weeks it had taken her to make this Friday-afternoon phone call.

"Sorry," he said—but she thought she heard a hint of amusement in his voice, and rejoiced. "Where do you want to go?"

"Back up in the hills beyond Delfield. There's some really pretty country there," Binky said, remembering Karen's description of Cameron as "semi-urban," and wondering if Piers had ever tried exploring the pockets of open countryside that still lay between the towns. "And at this time of year there should be lots of wildflowers in the fields that I've never seen before. I've done most of my painting in the woods. Well, I don't mean I always do the actual painting there, usually I begin with sketches and notes—" She felt herself floundering.

"I saw your exhibit in the library," he said unexpectedly. "Nice."

"Nice" was a word Binky detested, but never mind; in fact, coming from Piers at this moment it sounded rather beautiful. She hurried on. "Anyway, it's supposed to be a really great day tomorrow, and I thought if you didn't mind driving me, I'd pack a lunch for us, and . . . Do you like terrine?" She bit her lip, reminding herself that she hadn't meant to ask him that; let him find out when the time came. Besides, she'd spent all last night making the terrine, and she certainly wasn't going to leave it behind.

"I don't know," he said. "Never tried it. In fact, I don't even know what it is."

"It's a kind of pâté. I make it with veal and pork and

ham, and sometimes—" Binky stopped herself. Good grief,
she thought in vexation, why am I talking about recipes
when there's still the other important thing to say?

"Well, anyway, that's the first favor—driving me, I mean.
The second is, do you think you could bring your camera?
I'm a lousy photographer, and Karen said you were quite
good." If this got back to Karen, Binky hoped it would be
all right; in fact, she was pretty sure that was what Karen
had been about to tell her that night in the emergency room.
"Like I said, I'd be mostly sketching and making notes
about colors," she explained quickly, "but it would be really
great if I had some good color photos to work from, too."

For once Piers didn't hesitate. "Sure," he said. "I'd like
that."

"You would? I mean—well, that's great. Around ten,
then? Or ten-thirty, if that's too early," she added hastily.

"No. In fact, why don't we say nine-thirty? Get an early
start, in case it clouds over later."

Binky hung up smiling.

The morning smiled, too—a perfect Saturday in early
May, with soft blue skies and apple trees in bloom, other
trees just beginning to leaf out in a spectrum of delicate
greens pleasing to a watercolorist's eye. Binky hesitated for
a while over what to wear, then shook her head at herself
and put on jeans and a favorite old plaid shirt. At the last
moment she added a nylon Windbreaker.

Would Piers have borrowed his mother's Volvo wagon?
Binky hoped so. A tour of the countryside in a large gleaming limousine wasn't exactly what she had in mind, aside
from the fact that some of the back roads were pretty narrow. But when Piers drove up, it was in an old VW convertible, a car whose shape had always delighted Binky for some
reason. This one had recently been painted taxicab yellow,

and the top was down. Binky grabbed a scarf along with her sketchbook and the lunch basket, and ran down the walk.

"Great car!" she said. "Yours?"

"Mine. I've been saving up for it," Piers said, with what in anyone else would have been a proud, besotted grin. "I've always wanted a convertible," he confessed; and then added politely, "Do you mind having the top down?"

"Not if you don't mind having my hair tie itself up into a lot of little square knots," Binky said, deciding to dispense with the scarf. "Oh, I love it," she told him, patting the fender of the little car. "It's so sort of *cute*. But adventure-some-looking, too."

Piers shook his head at this description, but a smile tugged at the corners of his mouth. "Right," he said. "On to adventure. Which way?"

They had to take the Interstate for a few miles, which made conversation impossible between the rush of air, the noisy VW engine, and the thunder of passing trucks. But when Piers turned off at Binky's direction onto a secondary road heading north, she had a question ready.

"You said you saved up for the car," she said. "How? I mean, your allowance, or a job, or what?"

Piers shrugged. "A job, of sorts."

Binky told herself that her question had been a perfectly natural one, that she was not going to let Piers retreat into one of his silences. So she persisted: "Of sorts?"

His eyes on the road, Piers said, "Driving my dad's cars around. He pays me to do that. Not much—but it adds up."

He spoke stiffly. Binky said, "And you hate every minute of it, don't you?"

Piers shot her a startled glance. "I never said that. Most people would give their eye teeth to be cruising around in a new Continental, or whatever."

"But not you."

After a pause he muttered, "I just don't like being conspicuous, I guess."

Binky nodded. Satisfied with this exchange, she settled back, only to lean forward a moment later. "That's the turn we want, beyond the Texaco station. There's a fork just after it where we bear left."

And now at last they were in the country, on a narrow road running between level fields, some of them freshly plowed, some long since gone to seed where farmhouses stood empty with sagging porches and roofless barns. The sun blew warm on Binky's face; she tasted damp earth, the rich new grass, even (or so she told herself) the violets blooming thickly in the drainage ditches alongside the road.

"You're smiling," Piers said, with a sidelong look.

"I'm happy," Binky said simply, letting the smile go on. "I have a feeling it's going to be a wonderful day."

"Well, we've sure got the weather for it." But for a moment he laid his hand over hers—that familiar large square hand whose touch Binky now knew she had been missing for many long months. Then he slowed the car slightly, glancing up at the sky above a stand of willow trees. "Harrier hawk," he said, more to himself than to Binky. "Probably hunting field mice."

Binky knew what a hawk was, of course, but she didn't see how you could tell one kind from another when it was only a distant silhouette. She said so, and Piers explained about the length of the tail, how the wings made a V-shape in flight and were slightly raised instead of spread flat like those of most other hawks. Up close, he said, you'd see a white rump, and on young birds a reddish belly. In fact he went into the same kind of detail he'd given to describing football, but Binky found this a lot more interesting.

"I've always wanted to try painting birds," she told him, a bit shyly. "But not the stuffed kind. I mean, you *can* work that way, from exhibits. . . . But outdoors—well, they never stay in one place long enough for you to get a real fix on them. Even Audubon used to shoot or trap his birds and sometimes stuff them so he could see them in detail."

"Well, that's what's so great about photographs. If Audubon had had a camera . . ." Piers hesitated. "As a matter of fact, I've taken quite a few pictures of birds. You'd be welcome to them—to work from, I mean. Of course, they're Minnesota birds."

"Well, they can't be that much different from ours," Binky began, and then realized he was teasing her. She said a little defensively, "Who knows, we might even see an eagle today."

"An eagle?" Piers scoffed at her.

"There are quite a few golden eagles in this area, if you know where to look." Her father had pointed one out to her on their ill-fated hang-gliding trip, she remembered, with a familiar twinge of unease; not that they'd be going anyplace that high today.

The road had been climbing gently for some time, and now the fields had begun to tilt around them, broken in places by outcroppings of rock and patches of woods. Soon they could see the shape of hills against the sky ahead of them, a blurred uneven line against the blue.

"Nice," Piers said, shifting down as the grade steepened. "I didn't know there was so much—well, so much space still left around here."

"You really miss Minnesota, don't you, Piers?" Binky asked.

He nodded. She thought he wasn't going to say anything more, but after a moment he said slowly, "It was hard on all of us, moving back here. Not only because my dad's family has lived in Minnesota for generations, but because we were used to a small town where everyone knew everyone else.

Even Mom. I mean, she did grow up in the East, but just on a farm. . . . I suppose Cameron doesn't seem all that big to you, but to us—" He shrugged.

Binky said, "And I guess people aren't as friendly here as they are out West."

"I don't know about that. Busier, maybe. Anyway, it's different. And if you're shy, like Karen and my mom . . ." He concentrated on steering around a curve. "Well, you saw what it did to Karen. Back home she was class secretary and on the ski team, stuff like that. But here—well, it was like having to start all over, and I guess she just didn't know how to cope with that. If she couldn't be on the inside, she might as well stay on the outside . . . really outside, the way it turned out."

As casually as she could, Binky said, "And your mother . . . is that why she drinks?"

"Drinks?" Piers shot her a look of astonishment, almost driving off the road.

"Well, at the party . . . I thought . . ." Binky faltered. "But I guess it's none of my business," she said, using a phrase she'd resolved not to use today—or ever again with Piers, if she could help it, now that she understood that everything about him was, somehow, her business. But there would be a time and place, she reminded herself; don't rush things.

"Look," she said, pointing, glad of a distraction. "There's a place where we could leave the car."

Piers slowed and turned left onto the rutted track she'd spotted. It was barred after a few yards by an ancient barbed-wire gate, but there was room enough for the little car, and tangled vines would conceal it from the road. Beyond the gate a lush green upland meadow sloped away to their right, dotted with dandelions. Binky gathered up her sketchbook and the lunch basket, and then realized that although Piers had switched off the ignition, he hadn't taken his hands from the wheel.

In a tight voice he said, "Just what is all this about, Binky?"

Binky froze. "About? You mean about your mother? Look, Piers, forget I said that. I was just—"

"No. Today. This whole deal." He gestured angrily. "Your own mother's a photographer, isn't she? Why can't she take your flower pictures? *And* drive you, if your wrist is really still in such bad shape?"

Binky thought of saying that her mother hardly ever worked in color, that photography was just a business to her, that a busman's holiday was not her mother's idea of fun. Also that although her wrist was okay for things like carrying a lunch basket, it still hurt when she tried to grasp something like a steering wheel.

No. Those things were the truth, but not the important truth—and that was what today was all about.

"I wanted to get to know you better," she said.

Piers gave a short laugh. "Binky, we spent a lot of time together last fall, remember? And you're saying you don't *know* me?"

When she didn't answer, just looked at him, he fell silent. Then, suddenly, he slapped the side of the car and said harshly, "Okay. My mother. I guess I can see how you got the impression you did. But the fact is, she was terrified of giving that party. They didn't even *have* cocktail parties back home, and like I said, she's shy. She was afraid her dress was all wrong, that the house was all wrong, that the food was all wrong. She was practically paralyzed by fear the whole time."

"But why?" Binky said, before she could stop herself— one more question, and Piers might turn the car around and drive straight back to Cameron. "Why did she give the party, then?"

"For my dad," Piers said. "My big glad-handed, back-slapping dad, who decided the only way to make a success of the agency was to act like everybody's idea of a car salesman—make a big splash, live it up." More quietly, he explained, "The agency he had back home failed. There were a lot of reasons for that, including a superhighway and a shopping mall that were supposed to bring people into the area but that never got built. But Dad decided it was his fault, that he'd been too low-key, not aggressive enough or something. We weren't exactly in great financial shape, and so when he got the chance here . . ."

He drummed his fingers on the wheel. "The thing is, he really *is* a low-key kind of guy. His idea of a good time on Saturday night is tying some flies—for fishing," he explained as Binky turned a puzzled face toward him, "and playing chess. Instead of which he plays poker for stakes with the big shots these days. All part of the image."

Binky frowned, trying to reconcile this description of Mr. Anderssen with her own picture of a hearty, red-faced man with a glass in his hand.

Piers saw the frown. Surprisingly, he began to laugh. "You thought he was a drunk, too, I bet, didn't you, Binky? That glass he always carries around with him at parties . . . you know what's in it? Perrier. It looks like he's drinking gin or vodka—you know, one of the boys, which is the whole idea—but all that's in it is Perrier. Or sometimes club soda."

Binky digested this information, wishing Piers would stop laughing in that particular way. She shook her head and said, "I think that's sad."

Piers drew a deep breath and blew it out again in a sigh. "Yeah," he said. "It is. The whole thing is sad. And there's

more to it than that, deals I don't really know about—
nothing dishonest, I'm sure of that, just more role-playing,
but still . . . I don't know. The agency's doing really well.
Maybe after a while Dad will get his confidence back and be
able to relax. And then Mom will, too."

"Sure," Binky said. She laid her hand on his. "I'm sure
that will happen, Piers." He turned his head, and she saw
that his blue eyes were damp. "And you," she said softly.
"You played football when you came to Cameron because
. . . because that was your way of coping. And dated a
cheerleader for the same reason."

"Binky—"

"Later. We'll talk some more later," Binky told him. All
at once she found herself smiling again, she felt exhilarated,
light as dandelion fluff. "Do you realize we've just had a
real conversation, Piers? Our very first one." Before he
could say anything, she was out of the car, holding her face
up to the sun. "Wow, doesn't it smell good here? Come on,
get your camera. I think maybe I see a patch of gorse—or
do I mean broom?—there at the edge of the field. Those
yellow flowers—see?"

Piers sat regarding her for a moment. Then he shook his
head, climbed out of the car, and stood stretching for a
moment, as if he, too, felt a sudden sense of release. "You
are one crazy girl, Binky Nolan," he said, grinning at her.
"And those yellow flowers are just plain old wild mustard,
or maybe ragwort. Want to bet?"

Piers was right about the flowers, although Binky insisted
on checking her field guide to make sure. In fact, he knew a
great deal more about wildflowers than Binky did, as she
soon realized. After they'd wandered around the meadow
for a while in search of something more exotic than clover
and buttercups, he remarked dampeningly that early summer was really a better time for open-field flowers. (Well,

why couldn't he have told me that in the first place? Binky thought; and then answered herself, with a lift of her spirits: Because he wanted to come with me today, that's why.) He suggested they'd have better luck at the far side of the field, where a small stream ran under a windbreak grove of maples and oaks and poplars.

Again he was right. They found starflowers, hepatica, wild columbines, speedwells, even a misty, sky-colored patch of bluets. Some were familiar to Binky, others she knew only from pictures; Piers knew not only their common names but their botanical ones as well.

She also learned, somewhat less happily, that Piers was as much a perfectionist with his camera as she was with a paintbrush. Sometimes she'd completed several sketches in the time it took him to photograph a single plant.

"And I thought I was finicky," she said with a laugh, as Piers lay flat in the damp grass, shifting his body this way and that in order to get the best angle on a lady's slipper growing near the bank of the stream. ("A bit arty," he'd explained, "but this way you'll be able to see the whole shape of the flower.")

A few minutes later he was down on one knee in the streambed itself, shooting upward at a spray of Solomon's seal. Binky forbore to mention that she already had several paintings of Solomon's seal, which happened to grow plentifully in the woods behind her house. She stood on the bank with her sketchbook under her arm, trying not to look impatient.

But her face must have given something away, because Piers looked up at her and grinned. "You should see me when I go after birds," he said. "Once I spent three hours sitting in a thicket, trying to get a decent shot of a ruby-crowned kinglet. That was before I got a telescopic lens, which still seems like cheating, in a way. . . . Anyhow, just when I had the shot I wanted, it started to pour rain."

He clambered out of the streambed; and looking at him, Binky felt her momentary exasperation melt away. She saw a tall, rangy boy wearing a shapeless gray sweatshirt cut off at the elbows, worn green cord pants, muddy hiking boots. Burrs and tickseed clung to him, his cords were wet and grass-stained, his thick fair hair needed cutting. He looked hot and sweaty—but also eager, intent, almost radiant with energy. It was the same joyous quality Binky had felt in Piers on the football field whenever he broke free to run and spin and leap; but now the joy was in his face, too, open and unguarded.

This is Piers, she thought. This is really Piers at last.

"Speaking of rain," he said, squinting at the upper slopes of the meadow, where the grass gave way to a rocky escarpment, "it looks like we might get a shower before too long."

Binky followed his glance, but all she could see were a few fat clouds sitting above the hills to the northwest.

Piers said thoughtfully, "You know, I bet we'd find some alpines up in those rocks. Maybe not edelweiss, exactly, but stonecrops, saxifrage . . ."

Binky looked at the rocks rising into the sky. Oh, no, she thought. Please, no.

Misunderstanding her silence, Piers looked down at her sneakered feet and said, "You're not exactly dressed for climbing, I guess—but I'll give you a hand in the slippery places. Who knows," he teased, when she still said nothing, "we might even see your eagle from up there."

Binky looked at her watch and swallowed. "I thought maybe we should have lunch now," she said. Her stomach was fluttering, but not from hunger.

"Oh, come on. If it rains, it really could be tricky getting to the top. We can stash the lunch down below and eat when we get back down." He studied her face. "What's wrong?"

"I—I really don't like heights very much."

"Heights? Hey, it's not exactly a mountain, Binky, just a big rock pile. And like I said, I'll give you a hand if you need one."

Little do you know, Binky thought, struggling with herself. She'd always been fascinated by alpine flowers, the low-growing plants that bloom against all odds in barren places above the timberline. She knew them from pictures; some of them grew prettily in people's rock gardens. But she had never expected to see them growing in the wild, because of where they grew: up high. And high was where Binky never went—couldn't go. Not even with Piers. Or could she?

She looked up into his eager face. "Okay," she heard herself saying—recklessly, crazily. She added quickly, "But I warn you, you don't know what you might be getting into. I have a tendency to panic when I get up high. Sometimes I —well, I sort of freeze."

There: she'd said it. But lightly, too lightly (why, she thought miserably, can't I really *tell* him?), so that Piers obviously didn't take her words very seriously.

"If you freeze, I'll thaw you," he promised, with a smile that would have done so in ordinary circumstances. He moved away with his loping, long-legged stride. Binky closed her eyes for a moment in silent prayer, and then followed him.

11

Up close, the rock pile was steeper than it had looked from a distance, and also rougher—a tilted heap of broken granite that, Piers said, had been piled there by an ice-age glacier. (That's right, Binky thought numbly, as they started up, he knows about geology, too.) But there were pebbled strips of turf in the clefts between the rocks, and plenty of handholds, and the going wasn't really very hard, except for the last bit, where a trickle of water made the footing slippery.

"Watch it," Piers said, and reached down a hand to pull her up the last few feet. "So here we are. Hey, great view!" he said, shading his eyes to admire it; and added, "That wasn't so bad, was it?"

Binky shook her head. It wasn't climbing that bothered her, she could have told him, only looking back; looking . . . down. She kept her back to the view and quickly put some yards between herself and the edge. They were on a kind of rough plateau, where short tough grass grew among

weathered boulders and a few small wiry shrubs had rooted
themselves somehow in the gritty soil. Its rear wall was a
sheer rock cliff, the very sight of which made Binky shud-
der. At least he won't suggest climbing *that,* she thought.
Then her eye fell upon what appeared to be an iris in bloom
—except that it was only four inches high. With a cry of
delight, she fell to her knees. "Piers," she called, "I've got to
have a picture of this!"

They found miniature alliums, too, and sedum and
beardstongue, thymes and heathers. . . . Binky became so
absorbed that once or twice she even found herself facing
the dreaded view—the long green slope of the field, the belt
of woods dividing it from a parallel field in which sheep
grazed, the curving black ribbon of the road in the distance.
She told herself that it was beautiful, that after all there was
nothing like getting up high to appreciate nature in all its
variety, that her heart wasn't even beating fast, that she was
doing just fine.

Then Piers, with a glance at the sky, returned his camera
to its case, slung the strap over his shoulder, and said, "I
guess we'd better get a move on, Binky. It's going to pour
any minute. I'll go first, okay?"

He disappeared over the rocky lip of the plateau. Binky
made herself walk to the edge. And then it wasn't a lovely
pastoral scene she saw, it was a *drop*—a plunge of tumbled
rock, with the little pile of their gear visible way down at the
bottom, placed there as if to give scale; not that she needed
any.

I can't, she thought, and sat down abruptly, putting her
face in her hands.

"Binky?" Piers was calling her from below.

She felt the first raindrops strike cold through her cotton
shirt. So okay, she thought. I can stay here until I starve to

death or die of exposure. Or I suppose a helicopter could come pluck me off. Or—

The thing to do, she told herself in a tight little voice, is to turn around; to go down backward. That way you won't have to look. Never mind the trembling. Trust your body, which is strong and agile and trained in the art of balance. Balance . . . no, that was the wrong thing to think about. So stop thinking and just *do* it, she ordered herself.

Slowly her body began to obey her will. She squirmed around, clutching at a tough-rooted little cedar, and began inching her way down into the cleft. This was the slippery part, she reminded herself, feeling delicately with her sneakers for purchase on rough stones and pebbles, forcing herself to let go of the cedar. . . .

"Okay?" Piers, still just below her. "Good—that's the worst part. Now you can turn around."

That's what you think, Binky thought grimly, peering under her right armpit at a safe-looking ledge and stretching a foot sideways onto it. Now the other foot. On the ledge, okay. But now what? She was facing a smooth, tilted slab of rock, nothing to hold on to. With a gasp Binky spread-eagled herself against the slab, pressing all her weight into it. Anything to keep from standing upright, from feeling *space* around her.

"Binky, you can't come down backward all the way," Piers said. He sounded amused. But when she didn't move, he said more sharply, "Hey—turn around!"

"I can't," she said—but in the same moment she did, with a panicky flip-flop that somehow kept her body pressed back against the rock. She leaned into it, her eyes shut tight.

Over the hissing of the rain and the thick pounding of her heart Binky heard Piers' quick intake of breath. But when he spoke, his voice was calm. "Binky," he said, "I'm holding out a hand to you. You can reach it easily if you try. But first you have to open your eyes."

She shook her head. Even that small movement seemed to threaten her balance. "I'm afraid to look down," she said, forcing out the words between stiff lips.

"Then don't. Look at me. Keep your eyes on my face."

Piers' face. I love Piers' face, Binky told herself, and opened her eyes. His own were looking steadily up at her, as blue as the sky had been only a few minutes ago . . . a lifetime ago. Binky groped for his hand, not taking her gaze from his.

"Okay. Now take a step to your right. Then a step down. Turn a bit sideways—that's right. It gets narrow here, so I have to take my hand away, but just keep watching me. Do what I do. Take it slowly, easily. Pretend you're coming down a very short flight of steps. They're not even steep, and you're only a few feet above the ground . . . no, don't stop. Here's my hand again."

Somehow he managed to keep his head turned toward her as he picked his way down through the jumble of rocks and boulders. Her wrist hurt whenever there was a pull on her outstretched hand, but that was okay; the pain helped. Like a sleepwalker intent on a candle flame, her eyes never wavering from Piers' face, Binky followed. When he had to take his hand away again, he said, "Now you're beginning to relax a little—the rhythm is coming back. You know, that's the first thing I ever noticed about you, Binky, the rhythm in the way you move, as if you're always almost dancing. It's coming back now . . . can you feel it?"

Binky told herself she could, a little. Well, dancing, hardly; but at least there was a returning sense of her own body in familiar motion, a memory of balance and control. She even dared to take her gaze away from Piers' face for a moment—and saw that only a short, winding track remained now between the rocks and the blessed, almost-level grassy safety of the meadow. She looked back at Piers and saw that he was smiling at her.

"No wonder I feel better," she said shakily. "We're almost there!"

"But you were doing okay," Piers told her, and waited while she caught up with him. Now that the worst was over, her knees wanted to give way and her teeth were chattering. He put an arm around her and supported her the rest of the way, until she stopped stumbling and was able to walk almost normally again. "There at the end you were beginning to get over it just a little, don't you think?"

"I don't know. Maybe just a little. Oh, Piers!" Binky stopped and buried her head against him. "Thank you. I feel like such a fool."

He held her close. "I just wish you'd told me."

"I tried to, but—" Binky's throat tightened up; she was shaking again, and sobbing. Piers said nothing, just held her. Finally her muscles relaxed and she could speak again. "Ever since I was a little kid . . . and I hate it, I hate being afraid like that."

"It's nothing to be ashamed of."

"Yes, it is," Binky almost wailed. "And *that's* why I couldn't go skiing with you, why I told you that silly lie about frostbite—well, it isn't a lie exactly, I do have these peculiar toes, but—"

"I'm from Minnesota, remember? I know all about frostbite." His voice roughened. "I just thought you didn't want to be with me."

"Oh, I did. I wanted to be with you more than I even knew."

Binky realized she wasn't making much sense. She also realized that Piers was soaked through, and so was she, and that it was raining harder by the minute. She'd hardly no-

ticed the rain, coming down the mountainside (Piers could
call it a rock pile, but to Binky it was still a mountain).
"Our gear," she said dazedly, looking around for it. "The
lunch—my sketchbook—"

But luckily she'd thrown her Windbreaker down over the
sketchbook, and now she remembered that most of the food
was wrapped in foil. Still, they could hardly have a picnic
out here in the pouring rain—and suddenly Binky was rav-
enously hungry. If they could find some sort of shelter . . .

"Look," she said. "There's a kind of cave over there—
see, where those big rocks are tipped together. It looks
pretty dry underneath." She got down on her hands and
knees and crawled partway in. "Yes, it's almost like a tent,"
she called over her shoulder. "Bring the basket, will you,
Piers? You deserve a good lunch after all that, and I've even
got some hot soup. At least, I hope it's still hot."

Piers returned with the basket and pushed it in to her.
Binky wedged herself farther into the little cave to make
room for him, and began setting out food. "Good," she said,
opening a thermos, "it's still steaming. Chicken soup, Piers,
nothing exotic," she added with a grin. She filled a cup and
leaned to hand it to him. "Hey, you're still getting rained
on. Come on in, there's plenty of room."

He hesitated, then edged in a little way. Binky pushed the
basket to one side and tossed him her Windbreaker. "Here,
maybe you could drape this over the opening. It'll make
things kind of dark, but then the rain can't blow in."

Piers did as she asked, and Binky patted the stony ground
beside her. "Come on, move in a little more," she said, and
looked around in satisfaction. "Hey, it's sort of cozy in here,
isn't it? Nice." She unwrapped the terrine and broke off a
chunk. "You don't have to eat it if you don't like it—there's
some egg salad sandwiches, too, and I made us each a
strawberry tart. . . ." Binky was feeling better by the min-

ute. Chicken soup for what ails you, she thought with a smile, taking a long hot swallow.

She said, "You were really wonderful up there, you know, Piers? My father had to talk me down the side of a cliff once, but he sounded scared the whole time, and you were just so *calm*. . . . When I was up on top, all I could think of was how embarrassing it would be if they had to send a helicopter after me. You know, an air rescue like you see on TV, with bullhorns and medics and photographers and everything. And headlines: 'Girl Climber Panics.' "

Piers smiled, and took a sip of chicken soup. Binky saw him swallow hard. She also saw that he had that stiff, wooden look that had always made her so uneasy and that she'd thought was gone forever, at least when he was with her. In the dim light she made out, too, that he seemed to be sweating. . . . The hot soup?

"Piers?" she said. "What's wrong? Do you feel okay?"

He set his cup down. "No, not too good," he said. Abruptly he brushed the Windbreaker aside and pushed himself out of the cave. Binky scrambled after him in alarm. She found him standing out in the open with his head lifted to the rain, taking deep gulps of the wet air.

"What *is* it?" she said, clutching at his sleeve. "Piers, are you sick?"

He shook his head. Then he nodded, and forced a smile. "In a way, I guess. The same way you are. Except my problem isn't heights. It's being shut in."

"Claustrophobia," Binky said, suddenly remembering a lot of things that had puzzled her at the time. The way Piers always had to have the car window open, even in freezing weather, and doors or windows in small rooms, and—yes, the sick way he'd looked at the rock concert when they were crammed into their seats with all the exits sealed. . . .

"Mine's called acrophobia," she said.

"I know."

"Maybe you should have had your lunch up on top of the mountain. The rock pile, I mean. I could have packed two baskets." Binky began to laugh. She tried to stop herself, but the more she thought about the whole thing, the funnier it got—the two of them standing here in the rain with no place to go, or at least no place they could go together.

But Piers wasn't laughing, although he was breathing normally again. Sobering, Binky looked up at his wet face and said gently, "You told me my—my phobia was nothing to be ashamed of. Well, then, neither is yours."

He shrugged. "I'm like you, I guess. I hate being scared and not being able to do anything about it."

"But you *have* done something about it. I mean, you've fought it, whereas I've just—chickened out. By staying away from high places, I mean."

"Well, it's a little easier to avoid things like towers and mountains than it is to stay out of small rooms and closed-up cars and tunnels and stuff." No wonder he bought a convertible, Binky thought with a pang. "And you didn't chicken out today when I wanted to go climbing."

"Well—that depends on how you look at it," Binky said thoughtfully. "I guess I was more afraid of letting you know what a coward I was than of going up there. Until I got there, anyway." She shivered. "But look where I made *you* go—a cave, of all places."

Suddenly she was laughing again. "What a pair we turned out to be!" she said, and flung her arms around him. "Oh, Piers . . . do you think we could give each other therapy?"

"We could try," he said, rubbing his chin against the top of her head. She could feel that he was smiling at last. "Only maybe we should start on a little smaller scale. No more cliffs or caves for a while. I could help you with escalators, say, and you could help me with elevators."

"I should think elevators would be the worst," Binky murmured, lifting her face to his.

"They're bad, but at least they move. That helps, for some reason. Of course, if I ever got stuck in one . . ." He was kissing her eyelids now, the tip of her nose. "Promise you'll be with me if I ever get stuck in an elevator."

"I promise," Binky said against his mouth. And then for a while there was nothing in the world but Piers, the feel and smell of him, the sound of his heart thudding against her, the touch of his hands. . . .

"There's therapy and therapy," Binky said at last, tremulously, breaking away. "I think maybe this session better stop just about now."

"Why?" Piers said. But as he always had, he let her go; as always, they smiled at each other a bit sheepishly while they waited for the world to settle itself about them, to become familiar and solid and ordinary again. Or almost ordinary. . . .

As if on cue the rain slackened, flung down a last glittering shower, and stopped.

"Hey, the sun's coming out already," Binky said, and looked around. "See that nice flat rock over there? Let's bring the food out and have our picnic there."

"Food," Piers said, with a mock groan. "I might have known that's what you were thinking about. A one-track mind."

Binky shot him a look, and then grinned. "They go together—love and food. You just still haven't found that out. Did I ever tell you how crazy I am about cooking?"

"Well, I know you're crazy about eating—"

"Cooking," Binky said, and proceeded to tell him while they sat on the flat rock and had their picnic. Piers said cautiously that he thought the terrine might be an acquired taste, but praised the egg sandwiches (the trick, Binky told him, was a dash each of Worcestershire and French mustard, and just a pinch of chopped chives). She said she wanted him to come over for dinner some night soon. They'd have steak in his honor, but she'd do her Italian-fried onions—"you won't even know you're eating onions, Piers, they just *float"*—and maybe a Caesar salad. . . .

"Now that I know you better," she said seriously, "I think you'd really enjoy my family." And vice-versa, she thought. Even if she had to ply him with questions over the dinner table, she'd make him be the real Piers for them. But somehow she didn't think she'd have to.

Piers looked puzzled. "Well, I already like your parents. And as far as your brother's concerned—I guess he was jealous of me for a while, the way Karen was of you, but—"

"No, no, never mind Dennis. Dennis is easy. I mean, with Dennis, what you see is what you get. Even more so, now that he's taken up acting, if you know what I mean." Binky pondered the logic of this for a moment, and then shook her head. "But my parents—my mother the efficient career woman, my father the corporate executive. Conventional, conservative types, right?"

"Well—"

So Binky told him about her mother's treasure hunts among the town dumps, about her father's Evel Knievel weekends. From there, somehow, it was a natural step to talking about her feelings about art and about the kind of career she wanted (Piers listened intently, but Binky had a feeling Karen had already reported some of this to him). She told him about how she'd become a cheerleader more or less by accident, and about Spencer's machinations. "He was the one who came up with that dumb Supercouple label," she explained—and when Piers scowled, added, "But really, Spencer's not so bad. I think you'd like him if you got to know him." On second thought, she doubted if this were true. They were like members of two different species, Piers and Spencer.

Then, after a moment's hesitation, she told Piers about the sketch Karen had written.

"She really worships you, you know," she said. "Oh, Piers, stop scowling! Or no, don't. It's much better than having you go all blank and—and sort of stupid-looking, when really you're seething inside."

Piers looked a little taken aback at this; then thought about it, and grinned. "Still," he said, "Karen shouldn't have written all that stuff about me. I mean, that's my business. It's *private.*"

"Yes, but if I hadn't read it—" Binky looked away, making a business of rewrapping the few remaining scraps of their meal and returning them to the picnic basket. "Spencer says I have no imagination," she said slowly. "And I guess he's right. I mean, *I'm* a private person, but somehow I never expect other people to be, too. With you . . . well, I always knew there was something about you, but—"

Piers leaned to kiss her earlobe, and she pushed him away gently. "Something more than that, I mean. Though I was certainly jealous of Heather, and then of that—that—of Melissa Grant."

"Like I was jealous of Ted Fiske," Piers said, and Binky's heart gave a surprised little flip. "But something more . . . yeah, I know what you mean. I kept telling myself you were just a cute little cheerleader who liked a good time—parties and dances and rock concerts—"

"I hate rock concerts," Binky interrupted hotly. "I only went because of the other cheerleaders and because I thought you wanted to—and then, well, you were the big football hero, and I didn't see how I could let you down."

"And I only went because I thought you wanted to and I didn't want to let *you* down. I don't like that loud stuff, except sometimes outdoors."

"Yes, outdoors is okay," Binky agreed judiciously.

They looked at each other and laughed.

"Talk about lack of imagination," Piers said, shaking his head. He lay back on the rock, folding his arms under his head. "Heather was okay, but I don't know—boring, after you. And Melissa was . . . well, anything but boring, but *not* okay. As a person, I mean. That night at the basketball game—boy, now you see her, now you don't. No way she's going to get mixed up in something *sordid.* Not that I cared about anything after what happened to you."

"Oh, Piers." Binky sat looking down into his face, seeing there everything she'd missed before—the quickness and humor and sensitivity. She thought she'd like to try painting him sometime. Not that portraits were her forte; but still . . . "The thing with Ted was just marking time," she said, and stretched out beside him.

Piers took her hand and they lay gazing contentedly up at the sky, a clear, springtime blue once more. After a while Binky said, "You know, Piers, I am really not an *entertaining* sort of person." She felt him smile. "No, I mean it. I can go for hours without talking. Minutes, anyway. When I feel comfortable with someone."

To prove it, she said nothing at all for at least five minutes, giving herself up to the warmth of the sun on her face and the comfort, the rightness, of Piers beside her. She thought he'd fallen asleep until he said drowsily, "Hey, there was something I meant to tell you. About Doro Sprague."

"Doro?" For a moment Binky had to think who Doro was, that world seemed so far away.

"She does play the harp. In an all-girl orchestra over in

Livingston." Binky began to giggle. "True. Dad got trapped into going to one of their concerts—the daughter of some bank president plays in it, too. And there was Doro, looking like something out of an old painting, he said."

"What was she wearing?"

"He didn't say."

Binky smiled to herself. I bet it was chiffon, she thought; I hope it was. She closed her eyes.

Around them the rocks steamed in the sunshine and the grass of the meadow turned, if possible, an even brighter green. High above, something that might have been a golden eagle floated a moment on wide-flung glittering wings, circled once, and soared away.

About the Author

A graduate of Smith College, Mary Towne makes her home in Southern California. In Connecticut, where she lived for twenty-five years, she served as a consultant on the staff of the Institute of Children's Literature. Ms. Towne is the author of a number of books for young readers. Her most recent novel for Delacorte Press is *Paul's Game*.